Metaphorosis

August 2018

Beautifully made speculative fiction

Also from Metaphorosis Books

Reading 5X5: Readers' Edition
Reading 5X5: Writers' Edition

Best Vegan Science Fiction & Fantasy

Best Vegan SFF of 2017
Best Vegan SFF of 2016

Metaphorosis Magazine

Metaphorosis: Best of 2017
Metaphorosis: Best of 2016
Metaphorosis 2017: The Complete stories
Metaphorosis 2016: Nearly Complete Stories
Monthly issues

by B. Morris Allen

Susurrus
Allenthology: Volume I
Tocsin: and other stories
Start with Stones: collected stories
Metaphorosis: a collection of stories

Metaphorosis

August 2018

edited by
B. Morris Allen

Metaphorosis Books

Neskowin

ISSN: 2573-136X (online)
ISBN: 978-1-64076-114-8 (e-book)
ISBN: 978-1-64076-115-5 (paperback)

August 2018

The Bagel Shop Owner's Nephew

J. Tynan Burke

Last night, Murray called with another bunch of prophecies, so Yonatan Kaplan hasn't slept yet. He stayed up preparing dossiers on some doomed socialites instead. Now it's a little after dawn, Friday morning, and he's standing in line outside Fox's Bagels with a thermos and a tote bag. He's shaky from too much caffeine and too little sleep, but he doesn't regret it. The socialites will die this weekend, according to Murray, and Murray's got a good track record. When they do die, the obituary writers will call the Morgue—The Pre-Morgue Clipping Service, Yonatan's business—to buy the dossiers, expecting the usual thoughtfulness and prescience. So it had been best to begin the work immediately.

The line shortens when a gaggle of tourists leaves Fox's. Yonatan steps forward, fills his thermos lid with hot tea, and covers a yawn with the hand still holding the thermos. He thinks back to Murray's sneering tone when he 'apologized' for calling so late, his fake sadness that Yonatan would stay up all night working. It doesn't matter if Murray made a lucky guess or if it was knowledge from Murray's divine gift—either way, it's *rude* to mock a man for doing his job. Yonatan takes a big drink of tea and frowns. *Fucking prophets.* They're nothing like what you read about.

The line shortens again and it's Yonatan's turn to enter the shop. The woman in front of him holds the door, and he nods to her as he steps inside.

Yonatan is welcomed by a burst of humidity, which carries the smell of fresh onions and the accumulated yeast of three generations. He's also welcomed by a new cashier, a young man of maybe twenty who shares the owner Shay's big ears and too-skinny frame. The hunger in Yonatan's gut is replaced with a rarely-felt electricity, once debilitating, though he has learned to weather it. For him the closest analogy is the shock of a new and severe crush settling in, but he's not gay, trust him, he's checked.

This young man, whose name tag reads 'Stephen,' is perhaps a Tzadik Nistar.

"Morning," Yonatan manages, stepping to the counter. "One of everything, please."

Stephen raises an eyebrow over a baggy eye. "Like, one everything bagel, or..."

Yonatan cringes and tries to twist it into a smile. "Sorry. Bad joke I have with Shay. One of each kind of bagel, please."

Stephen counts off on his fingers. "So one plain, one poppy, one sesame, one onion..."

"And one everything," Yonatan finishes.

Stephen collects and bags the bagels. "I don't get it."

Yonatan shrugs. "I said it was a bad joke. Is it even a joke? Who knows how these things start." Yonatan knows. He tried making a pun five or six years ago after a long night of drinking. "Shay might remember. Do you know Shay, uh..." He points at the name tag like he just noticed it. "Stephen?"

"Uncle Shay? I sure do. It's Steve, though. That'll be fifteen dollars." Steve beeps some buttons on the register.

"You know what, Steve, why don't you add another poppy."

Steve wraps the extra bagel while Yonatan observes. No piercings or ink that he can see. That's good, it's one of the rules Adonai actually cares about any more.

The register beeps again. Steve says, "Eighteen dollars."

Yonatan hands him a twenty and puts the bagels in his tote. "Nice to meet you, Steve. Tell Shay Yonatan says hi."

Out front, Yonatan leans against the wall and takes two deep breaths while his gut settles. It turns to growling, sour with too much tea and too little food. Much better, easy to address. He returns to the Morgue and goes straight to the computer, where he opens a password-protected document and types an addition to a long list of names, in a column headed 'CANDIDATES': *Stephen 'Steve' Fox, ~20, Lower East Side, NYC.* And then, at long last, it is bagel time. Poppy, toasted, with leftover veggie cream cheese.

Later he's on the office couch, taking a little break and reading a space opera, when the landline rings. It's barely audible over the Norwegian black metal he put on to stay awake. His watch says eight-thirty, but he decides to take it anyway—it can't be any less interesting than the exposition dump he's at in the book, or the *Page Six* profiles he's avoiding. Off goes the music and in goes a bookmark. The bookmark has an Emerson quote he likes. He can read part of it sticking out: *Time and space are but physiological colors which the eye makes, but.*

While he crosses the Morgue, he steps over a spilled pile of clippings, and growls. Always more work, dossiers to build, Tzadikim to chronicle, things to file. Sleep, somewhere in there. And the phone keeps ringing, and he almost yells something passive-aggressive at it, but no, that's more something his father would do. With a silent glance back at the clippings he walks the rest of the way.

"Pre-Morgue Clipping Service, this is Yonatan."

"Thank you for answering, Yonatan. I hope it is not too early." A woman, British? Her voice seems far away, like a long-distance call in some old movie.

Her comment reminds Yonatan that he stayed up all night, and he stifles a yawn. "It's no trouble at all, Ms..."

"How rude of me. My name is Ariel."

Like the mermaid? Yonatan thinks. He can't help himself—he's never met a woman with that name before. He gets a stupid grin at the idea of talking to a cryptid.

"How can I help you, Ariel?"

"I am looking for somebody, of course."

Yonatan clears his throat and recites a spiel. This happens. "I'm sorry, Ariel, but this isn't that kind of place. We do collect information on people, but we don't release it until they're deceased. I can refer you to several good private investigators."

A pause, then Ariel continues. "Yes, of course, how silly of me—he *is* deceased. Or that's what I've heard. I was hoping you could tell me, and then if... I am looking for his remains."

Yonatan bites his lip. This feels like the sort of thing that will involve lawyers, maybe family drama. He should have let it go to voice mail. "Why don't you tell me who you're looking for, and leave me your contact information, and I'll get back to you," he says, a little too quick, to get her off the line. He wonders if the machine that records his calls is still working. He hasn't had to check in a while.

"I'm sorry, have I said something wrong?" She sounds sweet, like she doesn't know.

And maybe she doesn't, maybe there's a language barrier or Yonatan is maybe cranky. A saying of his mom's pops into his head, *Make sure to offer somebody an offramp before they drive too far down stupid street,* so he does. "Did you mean to say you're looking for his *grave,* instead of his *remains?*"

Another pause. "That is probably the better word. We wish to pay our respects."

"Alright." He explains the fee structure, and takes down a credit card number and the name of the man in question: John Miller, possibly died 'quite recently', near San Francisco. It startles him—that's the name of a Tzadik Nistar. And about a million other people, of course. Anyway, last he checked, John the Tzadik was alive and living in San Diego. Still, something feels off about Ariel, so after he hangs up, Yonatan decides to download the call from the recorder. He finds the device inside a junction box by the front door, warm and smelling like hour-old tar. It's fried. His assistant Sarah comes in a minute later while he's digging in the wiring with a flashlight between his teeth. He turns and asks for help, and accidentally blinds her.

While they extract the recorder together, he brings her up to speed on the socialites' dossiers. Could she pick up where he left off, and also run to the gadget store for a new recorder? There're fresh bagels in the kitchenette. He grabs his space opera and goes home without telling her about Ariel's call. She doesn't need to know, she isn't a Searcher. From the privacy of his apartment, he sends an email to the Searcher who follows Miller, checking in. Finally he goes to bed.

Asleep, he dreams—who doesn't? Sometimes he has one of the dreams everybody gets, like having a test he forgot to study for even though grad school was six years ago. Once he had an entire month of dreams where every day was Saturday and he had to follow his dad's Shabbat rules, which he never had to in real life. His dad didn't go all Haredi—instead of 'Haredi' you can say 'ultra-orthodox,' if you want to piss his dad off—until after the terrorist attacks really started to ramp up in America, around when Yonatan was starting college.

This morning's dream is about a maple tree. He's squatting on a crook in the branches, up where the trunk first splits, with a magnifying glass and a clipboard. The clipboard holds a chart, the scientific names of bugs on the left and numbers on the right. He's a scientist doing a population survey. He counts tiny black ants through the magnifying glass, writes the number next to their species name. The name's in Latin, and he wishes he knew how to pronounce—

Of course he knows how it's pronounced, he's been studying liturgical languages for years. This is a dream. He straightens out his back and stretches. Even here, it hurts from all the time he spends at his desk. He should really get a better chair.

"What are you doing? Don't just squat there if you aren't going to work."

Yonatan looks down. The source of the voice is a park ranger in iridescent green, like a beetle with a chip on its shoulder, gender indeterminate. While the ranger glares, Yonatan inspects some leaves. Aphids are munching on the cellulose while lady-bird beetles munch on the aphids. He's too distracted to count them, so he hops onto the grass and brushes crumbled bark off his shirt.

"I guess it's time to go, then," he says, pocketing his magnifying glass.

"I guess so," says the ranger.

"What'd I do wrong?"

"I just don't like people climbing in my tree when they don't have a good reason." The ranger puts their fists on their hips, a superhero pose.

"Just this tree?"

The ranger spreads their arms. "There aren't any other trees."

Yonatan sees he's in a field, wild grasses stretching to the horizon. He looks up at the maple appreciatively. It's well-pruned and healthy. "You must be very dedicated to your work," he says.

"We all do what we must." The ranger rolls their eyes and bows. "But seriously though, thanks for your part. Now get going."

Yonatan nods, climbs into the Ford Explorer he hasn't owned for ten years, and drives off to the lab.

He wakes and showers, and by the time he's finished, the sun has set and it's Shabbat, the Jewish day of rest. Many in his neighborhood, inside the old borders of the Manhattan *eruv,* observe it; a quick glance out his apartment's paint-flecked window confirms their absence on the streets. Yonatan rarely observes; he's usually busy with Searcher work, and today is no exception. The only concession he makes is accessing the office remotely, which is not really a concession at all. He looks back at his laptop, at an email from Sarah. Executive summary: she finished the socialites' dossiers and got a new call recorder set up. The old one only broke that morning, so they have Murray's call, but nothing after.

Yonatan goes to make a cup of tea and heat up some leftover beef *pad see ew.* The tea is black and steeps in his favorite mug, also black, to match his jeans and hoodie—*even your favorite **tea** is black,* his dad jokes. Text on the mug reads *The Chosen Son.* It's half-blasphemous, a birthday present from his mom a few years ago. *Shh, don't tell your father,* she said with a wink. They're still together. He'll never understand it. Carrying his dinner back to his computer, he stubs his toe, and narrowly avoids saying "God damn it," choosing instead the more respectful "Fuck!"

There's a reply in his inbox with bad news about John Miller. During a business trip to San Francisco this week, Miller was beaten into a coma. He died of his injuries just this morning. Yonatan blinks twice. He hopes that Ariel wasn't asking about *that* John Miller, but can't really convince himself it's a coincidence. Then he reminds himself that people usually call right after a death—it's the Morgue's whole business model. Difference is, nobody ever asked him about one of the Tzadikim before.

To still the dread creeping over his scalp, he plugs his phone into his sound system and resumes the Norwegian metal playlist. The part of him that isn't freaking out hopes it annoys the upstairs neighbors. They're always clomping around at four in the morning. What are they, meth heads?

He sets a couch cushion on the floor and sits, closing his eyes and counting breaths. He wishes there were a Searcher manual to consult, but theirs is an oral tradition, a secrecy born from the historical necessity to hide. The next best thing would be to ask Leonard, his old mentor and thesis advisor, but Leonard's been dead almost a year. Upon reflection, Yonatan knows Leonard would just repeat the fundamental rule about Searching: *If somebody asks for information about a Tzadik Nistar, you must provide it.*

Yonatan's no good at following rules he doesn't grok the need for, but the rationale behind the rule is obvious, to somebody who knows the history. His thoughts go to his first real Searcher meeting. It was in a faculty bar that the university had shoved into a basement.

"So you've passed the hard part of the test," Leonard had said. "Now for the oral portion. Explain, in your own words, the Tzadikim Nistarim."

Yonatan nodded. "An old Talmudic legend. Thirty-six righteous people who are so great, they keep God from trashing this place. If some day only thirty-five people held that honor, God would wipe us out."

Leonard tut-tutted. "Please, use one of the other names, around me at least."

"Does... Adonai actually care?" The word felt funny in Yonatan's mouth.

"There are things Adonai cares more and less about. The work I do with the Tzadikim, securing the life of creation—it's more important than, say, Shabbat, if you need it to be. But Adonai's name is a matter of basic respect."

Yonatan glanced at his vodka tonic. "Sorry, Leonard. I'll work on it."

"Thank you. So these Tzadikim Nistarim, they're special?"

"One could even be the Messiah," Yonatan said. "A Tzadik Nistar doesn't know they're a Tzadik Nistar. Some say it's a metaphor to encourage you to behave well—you never know when you might turn out to be one."

Leonard waved his hand. "But..."

"But you say they're real."

"I don't say, Yonatan, I know. And I know you can feel it—you picked one out of a full lecture hall."

Yonatan grunted. Both men sipped their vodkas. Leonard put a hand on the table. "Eschatology aside, the archive is still a brilliant career opportunity, you know. I'm old, and I need an apprentice. And—this is just a personal observation— I don't see academia in your future."

Yonatan snorted and then agreed. So began his life with the Searchers, who identify and chronicle these Tzadikim, and provide information about them whenever it's requested. Yonatan jokes that it's in case Adonai ever loses his phone book. And they have a simple principle: *always provide the information.* After all, you never know who might be asking.

Well, as Leonard liked to remind him, one has principles so one can follow them in uncertain situations. Thinking about the present, Yonatan adds, *But that doesn't mean one has to like it.* This situation is uncertain as fuck. Miller was *murdered.* Why is Ariel drawing his attention to it? She doesn't *sound* like a prophet, or not like any he's talked to. More importantly, has somebody begun knocking off the Tzadikim? He hopes not —it's onerous enough locating the replacement when just one has died.

He can only see malign interpretations... but maybe that's just him. Breathing, he knows that he doesn't actually need the answers to do his job. All he *has* to do is get Ariel the information on Miller, and follow the procedures for when a Tzadik Nistar dies: Adonai will give a different righteous person a promotion, and the Searchers will re-examine their Candidates. They'll check their premonitions from afar, and consult the prophets; if there's sufficient evidence about a Candidate, people will follow up in person and see how they feel.

Then, like so many things, it will conclude with an argument on the Internet.

Yonatan stands and returns to the table.

While he picks at his noodles and finishes his tea, he contemplates his tepid mug. *The Chosen Son.* When he's done eating, he goes to the Morgue to pull Miller's file.

An NYPD detective surprises him at the Morgue around eight. She introduces herself, Detective Corazón Lopez, can she come in and ask some questions? Yonatan flashes guiltily to the documents about Miller he was scanning, but he hasn't done anything wrong, he doesn't even know why the detective is here. Even so, he wants to tug nervously at his collar like Bugs Bunny, but he hides it, says yeah, asks if she wants some water or tea. She says no, and so he doesn't get anything for himself either. They sit at the card table in the kitchenette.

"An interesting business model," Lopez says, "selling dead person facts."

"Newspapers used to have departments like this," Yonatan says. "Probably half our archive is stuff we picked up from the *Times* when it went under."

"I did not know that." Lopez produces a notepad from her tan leather jacket and jots something down. "You oughta put that on your website."

Yonatan frowns. "Takes some of the mystique out, don't you think?"

Lopez smiles back. "Might make people like me less *curious*. Don't you think."

What is this? Yonatan shows his palms. "Can I help alleviate that curiosity?"

"That's the idea." Lopez looks out of the kitchenette, at the room of rolling stacks, the hallway down the middle crammed with file cabinets and banker's boxes. Her shoulders relax and she leans in. "Alright. There's been some suspicious deaths these last few months. Medium-profile, local celebrities." She's clearly not talking about Miller, which only barely reduces Yonatan's anxiety. "One of us noticed that the obits came out pretty quick, pretty detailed, like they'd been researched beforehand. We called the writers, they told us about you."

Yonatan nods, his mouth dry now, and he wishes he'd gotten water after all. "It's what I—we—do, detective. We identify notable and interesting people and prepare dossiers. Sometimes they die unexpectedly, and that's when we're most in demand. It's morbid, but it's a niche we proudly fill." He hopes the normalcy of business-speak is as comforting to her as it is to him.

"You seem to get awful lucky. Look, we know you solicit tips about people to profile, it's right there on your website."

He scrunches his face. "And the NYPD thinks a tipster might be involved in this?"

She shrugs. "Sounds crazy, right? But it's worth looking into. We think they're all the same perp, and you're linked to them too in your own way. We were hoping you could tell us about the tipsters."

"We have a policy against that."

It's Lopez's turn to show her palms. "You wouldn't want to seem uncooperative, would you? And do you have any idea how easy it would be to get a warrant?"

He doesn't, but pissing off the cops does seem riskier to the Morgue than compromising on this, and there are no Searcher rules about the prophets. "Sure. Alright. Give me the names of the deceased and I'll see if anybody mentioned them to us."

She does. The computer says they're all names from tips, all tips from Murray. He explains it to her, and she takes it down, standing behind him while he works.

"Does Murray have a last name?" she asks.

"Probably, but I don't know it."

"Do you at least have his *phone number*?"

"I do... he called last night, actually." Yonatan deflates. "He gave me three names, some local socialites." Maybe he shouldn't mention the details, that Murray said they won't last the weekend. He doesn't want to get the police involved in knowing the future, he's seen that old movie *Minority Report*. But human life is sacred, certainly more so than company policy, even this company.

"I have a recording," his conscience helpfully adds for him, settling the matter. His brain catches up and he says, "I should warn you, Murray thinks he's psychic. He says lots of crazy stuff... and he said they might die this weekend."

Lopez stares at him like he admitted he has bodies in the freezer, but don't worry, he has a permit. "*So* hard to find good help. Can I *get* the recording?"

Yonatan stiffens. "I need to know I'm not liable for anything, that the Morgue— that's what we call it, I know, I know—

isn't in trouble, or else you'll need that warrant."

"Mister Kaplan, these people could be in danger." She sighs and takes out her phone. "The D.A. is working tonight. You got a lawyer we can hammer something out with?"

Yonatan copies down a phone number from the computer. His lawyer keeps Shabbat, no work and no phone calls, but his assistant can fetch him. Lopez trades her business card for the number. "Have the D.A. call this—it's my lawyer Joel's assistant Kacy. Tell her Yonatan Kaplan says to get Joel ASAP, it's a matter of life and death."

After Lopez leaves Yonatan sinks his face into his hands, tugs on his hair. This is more murders than he's used to dealing with on a Friday night, which is zero. He needs a drink and something that wasn't cooked yesterday. Randomly he texts the woman he's newly dating, Dinah. She gets right back to him, she's free. They meet at a diner off 1st Avenue that smells like frying sausage and somebody else's Tabasco.

"Every time we eat you get steak," Dinah says when their food arrives, his steak and eggs, her Greek salad.

"I like steak," he says. He takes a bite and finishes his beer. "I used to be a vegetarian, did you know that?"

"I did not," she says.

"I had a Buddhist phase starting in undergrad. Ate a lot of hummus."

"A real rebel." Dinah eats some of her salad and drinks her own beer.

"You have no idea." Yonatan flags down a waiter and orders another drink.

"Why'd you stop? Being vegetarian," she says.

"It was *hard*," he says with a forced whine.

She laughs. "And a Ph.D. wasn't?"

"Different hard. When you find the right thing to care about, something that clicks..." He shrugs.

"I hear ya."

While they eat, Yonatan's mind keeps drifting to Ariel, and to dealing with the cops, and he keeps shoving the thoughts down. He's only half surprised when he blurts out, "What are you doing after this?"

Dinah smiles. "Nothing, you?"

"I'm in a whiskey-and-cartoons kind of mood," he says.

Dinah looks into her empty beer glass. "It'll have to be your place, they're fumigating my neighbor's, ew."

"My TV isn't very big," Yonatan says.

She puts her hand on his, says with a fake, over-earnest tone, "It's not the size that matters, it's the company."

The door is unlocked when they get to his apartment, and when Yonatan turns on the light he finds the place trashed—books and clothes everywhere, the kitchen table turned over, his not-very-big TV smashed. Dumb as a cow, he walks inside. "What the fuck!"

Dinah stays put in the door frame. "I assume it's not normally like this."

"No..." Yonatan holds up a hand and searches the apartment to confirm it's empty. It doesn't take long, it's not that big. "You can come in if you want. Try not to touch anything."

She looks relieved. "Oh, thank god. I gotta piss but it seemed like a bad time to ask."

He points her to the bathroom, and while she's in there he does a more thorough search. There's a note on the fridge, scrawled on the back of an envelope. *Murray says hi.* Dinah joins him while he's staring at it.

At the same time, they both say she should leave, and they share a sad laugh. She zips up her coat. "This wasn't a very good date, Yoni."

"I'll do better next time." He's already got his wallet out, rummaging for Lopez's card.

"You better." She kisses him, quick but not a peck, and leaves.

Yonatan jams the door shut and calls the detective. She picks up and says that Joel should call any second to fill him in. Yonatan tells her about his apartment, about the note. She says she'll send somebody over. His phone beeps, and he switches calls.

"Joel? Hey, before we start, uh…" Yonatan tells Joel about the break-in.

After a pause, Joel takes a few false starts and sighs. " 'Well, here's another nice mess you've got me into!' What was that, Laurel and Hardy?" Joel makes ancient references when he's nervous.

"Never watched it. I don't suppose you can tell me everything's gonna be okay?"

"Right, sorry." Yonatan hears Joel flipping through papers. "Honestly I can't see how the break-in changes anything on my end, for this Murray business. You're fine, legally. The cops weren't bluffing about the warrant though, that would be easy to get, so you had the right instincts, to cooperate. Judges don't like being pulled in after hours." A little edge of resentment to Joel's voice at the end. "So you're fine, and the Morgue is fine, but you should probably get used to hearing from law enforcement more. They're jealous of your tip line."

Yonatan grunts. Half the Morgue's revenue must come from prophets' tips, prophets who are usually shady as fuck, who'd bolt at the first sign of the cops. But saving lives is the right thing to do. Hopefully he'll only scare away people who are trying to pass murder plots off as revelations. Then again, what if the murder plots *are* the revelations—? Best not to go down that road, not sober at least.

"Oh, one more thing," Joel says. "They want you to call Murray so they can get a trace."

Fucking fuck. "I don't really want them to hear... *I* don't really want to hear what he has to say, even."

"Is this about your, er, *other* archive, Yonatan?"

Joel isn't a Searcher, but Yonatan's told him about it. Joel just thinks it's a run-of-the-mill weird sect. Spilling Adonai's secrets is unwise, but so is keeping secrets from your lawyer. Yonatan rubs the back of his neck with his free hand. "Yeah, and Murray's not making us look good."

More paper-shuffling on Joel's end. "I'll write it up so the cops can only use or store information pertaining directly to the investigation. They hear weird stuff all the time anyway. Well, not weird, but, you know."

"Unusual," Yonatan says, his old offramp tic.

"Yeah."

"Joel? Sorry I made you break Shabbat," Yonatan says.

"I'm not in love with it either, but hey. You're not the first client who's done it, but you *are* the first in a long while that I'm not mad at for it. I'll talk to the D.A. and sort out the paperwork we'll need to get you through the weekend. You and I can talk insurance and everything Monday."

"Great. Thanks."

"You got somewhere you can stay?" Joel says.

"I'll probably end up at the Morgue tonight. Worst case there's always my parents'."

"Oof."

Yonatan says goodbye and starts packing an overnight bag. Over by the wall he finds his mug—still intact, lucky him—and the space opera he's been carrying around. The bookmark's fallen out of the novel, and he can see the full Emerson quote now: *Time and space are but physiological colors which the eye makes, but the soul is light: where it is, is day; where it was, is night; and history is an impertinence and an injury if it be anything more than a cheerful apologue or parable of my being and becoming.* Now is not the time to figure out what chapter he was reading, so he slots the bookmark in under the title page, and puts the book in the bag.

At the Morgue some hours later, Detective Lopez and two techs sit at the card table with bulky headphones, and Yonatan leans against the wall, shoulders clenched, cordless phone pressed to his ear.

"So you got a pretty big mouth, huh?" Murray says when he answers. "You get my message? The cops there right now? 'Cuz I'll hang up."

Yonatan has practiced this in his head. He pretends to humor Murray's 'delusions.' "Wouldn't you know if they were?"

"You sound tense. Guess my friend's visit did that." Yonatan hears a *snap!* like Murray is chewing gum. "But I know you wouldn't talk about this in front of the cops. Don't even have to use my gift."

For once, it's a good thing that Murray is an asshole. Yonatan holds back something sarcastic. "So what is it you want?"

"A little loyalty, please," Murray says. "How much money have I made you guys with my tips? And all so selflessly."

"What's going on, Murray?"

"I give you names, right? Most of them are, ah, preordained. But every so often, some of them... I know a guy who wants you to know those names."

Yonatan squints at nothing, confused. "Why?"

There's the snapping sound of gum again. "He's *in love* with these people, but all fucked-up like. He wants them to die beautiful, right, so they gotta die soon. And he wants them to have a real good obituary. He knows about you guys somehow, used to write at a paper I think, he's a fan of your work. Well before he knocks 'em off he has me call you, to make sure all the research is in the can."

Murray pauses to chew wetly, then continues, "You should take it as a compliment, Yoni! Look, just *chill,* okay? Think how many of those weirdos I've, what'ya call it, *revelated,* for your little side project."

A headache tightens around Yonatan's crown, and he puts more weight against the wall. He looks at Detective Lopez and sees her looking back at him. *Keep him talking,* she mouths, and shrugs like this is a normal sort of evening for her. Maybe it is.

"Is that some kind of threat?" Yonatan says.

Murray laughs. "Like anybody would believe me if I told them, or even *care* about your little list. Lemme tell you something."

Yonatan clears his throat and swallows what comes up. "Okay."

"I'm a slimy little card sharp, but *you...*" Murray laughs. "I'm dirty, yeah, but I really *can* see the future too, and *you're* the one who thinks you've got a direct line upstairs? On account of some old legend? You know where I see *you*? The fuckin' *nuthouse*."

Silence. If it was just Yonatan he'd hang up, unplug the phone, and go make some bad decisions at a bar. But he's got a job to do, so he repeats himself, stalls for time. "Is that a threat? What is it you *want*?"

Murray chuckles. "Hey, *you're* the one who called *me*."

Yonatan looks and sees Lopez giving him a thumbs up with one hand, and miming hanging up with the other.

"You know what? Never mind. Go fuck yourself, Murray." Yonatan ends the call and swings the phone down, pressing it into his leg.

Lopez walks over. "Well done, Mister Kaplan," she says, sticking out her hand.

Yonatan stands up straight and shakes it. "Thanks. Uh, I could really..." He releases her grip and flaps his hand around aimlessly, noticing a tremor in his fingers.

She nods. "Gotcha. Don't disappear, OK?"

He folds his arms and nods back, realizing halfway through that it makes him look like the genie from that old TV show. The techs undo whatever they did to his phone line as he watches, and right before the door closes behind them, he remembers to call out his thanks.

He can't go home, so he does his best to make the Morgue comfortable, unpacking his book and changing into pajamas. He boils filtered water to make tea. A peek in the paper bag from Fox's shows that Sarah left him the second poppy-seed bagel, which he toasts and eats with butter. He finds where he was in the novel and, until his hands stop shaking, he reads. Then he works, cataloging the spilled clippings he noticed that morning, and pondering Ariel. It feels like he might know even less about that situation than he did a few hours ago. He resolves to consult other Searchers before he reaches too many conclusions. Meanwhile, the very next step is clear. He copies Miller's file, removes the Searcher-related information, and adds the police and coroner's reports he was sent.

That done, he yawns and lays down on the couch. He must've fallen into a dreamless sleep, since when he wakes up to the ringing phone, it's light out. With all that's going on, he figures he should answer.

"Pre-Morgue Clipping Service, this is Yonatan."

"Thank you for answering again, Yonatan, and on a Saturday." It's Ariel. He recognizes the accent, and the far-away sounding connection.

"How can I help you?"

"I know it has only been a day, but I was wondering if you were able to get the information on Mr. Miller for me."

"I was," Yonatan says. "I'm sorry to say that Mr. Miller has passed. I can email our file to you right after I run your card, if you'd like."

"Dreadful news. And I would appreciate that very much. You're fast—you must be very dedicated to your work."

He raises his eyebrows. "We all do what we must," he tries.

"Yes, and thank you for your part." Ariel sighs. "I have more people to check on... hopefully the news will be better. It's almost three dozen names, so I'll use the email form on your website, there's no rush. And..."

She hesitates, and Yonatan swallows.

"One last question," she says. "I see that you take suggestions for interesting people to research?"

"That's right. You get a finder's fee after their information's requested, if you were the first to suggest them."

"Well. You should keep an eye on a young man who's just moved near you, Stephen Fox. Consider this free of charge —I imagine he'll be around long after you're gone. Have a good Saturday, Mister Kaplan."

The line goes dead. Yonatan can smell burning plastic. The recorder must have gotten fried again. He takes a few calming breaths and flexes his fingertips out, deciding he can deal with all this tomorrow or maybe Monday. Meantime he's earned a break. He disconnects the dead recorder from the phone line, and then disconnects the phone entirely. For now he'll read his book uninterrupted; if Adonai has truly chosen this gray morning to count his Tzadikim Nistarim, he can always knock.

See J. Tynan Burke's story "The Bagel Shop Owner's Nephew" online at Metaphorosis. If you liked it, leave a comment. Authors love that!

Remember to subscribe to our e-mail updates so you'll know when new stories are posted.

About the story

Late last year, an acquaintance recommended the documentary 'Obit,' about the obituary department at the New York Times. I was struck by the frazzled archivist who runs the clippings morgue. At the same time, I was flipping through Borges's 'Book of Imaginary Beings,' and found an entry on the Tzadikim Nistarim (which Borges called 'Lamed Wufniks'). So I thought it would be interesting to write a story combining the two, about a frazzled archivist who runs an obituary-shop-slash-apocalypse-prevention-directory.

As for the rest of the story, I honestly don't know where these things come from. A surprisingly high percentage of my good ideas come to me when I'm trying to fall asleep. Very few come in the shower.

Finally, I have my lovely beta readers to thank for a few details and story beats, as well as for making the story much better than it would have been if they hadn't given me notes.

A question for the author

Q: What is your favorite part of writing?

A: At the craft level, I really enjoy writing dialogue. On a macro level, my favorite part is having created stories that my friends (and people like them) enjoy reading. If I hadn't written them, they're probably stories I would enjoy reading, too. Unfortunately, there's a lot of hair-pulling involved in the final product, and I need some distance before I can try to appreciate the result.

If you consider reading to be a part of writing, then I like that a whole lot, too.

My least-favorite part, not that you asked, is fixing plot holes.

About the author

J. Tynan Burke is a digital librarian and writer. He lives in San Francisco with his husband and their enormous cat.

www.tynanburke.com, @tynanpants1

Upon the Fallen Leaves of the Ginkgo Tree

Mads Alvey

To walk upon the fallen leaves of the Ginkgo tree is very nearly to walk upon a river of gold. It is a sight of such pure beauty that the Speakers whisper sweet blessings to the earth, spinning a preservation upon the leaves where they lie, so the golden carpet won't fade to black as we tread upon the ground.

I was reminding myself of how lucky I was to have enough Speaking to join the Speakers of the Ginkgowood when Amber chastised me during a Speaking lesson. The Speakers were the people who made my home such a beautiful spectacle, and I needed to remember that it was an honor to join them. My Speaking was a gift from the Ginkgowood, a power that had come to me without rhyme or reason as a child, which I needed to make the most of. What would I do with the neighborwood's gift, aside from use it?

"You can't ask it to go against its nature," Amber said, rubbing her temple.

The branch on which I sat was just as completely populated with yellow, fan-shaped leaves as it had been that morning. "It's fall!" I replied, calling down to her. "I'm asking it to grow apples, even though it's the wrong time of year, and it's the wrong type of tree. I don't know how this goal is anything *but* against its nature."

Amber sighed. "You have to think of this differently," she said. "A ginkgo tree and an apple tree are both trees; they both bear fruit. You're asking it to imagine that it is a different type of tree, that's all."

I frowned. "And the fact that it's fall?"

"You're asking it to come to harvest soon, that's what it already does in the fall," she said with a shrug. I was used to Speaking branches into different forms, but this was the first time I'd tried Speaking a tree into doing something new.

Amber had reminded me before I climbed onto the branch that it was the same principle; I was asking the life's essence to do something, but that didn't mean it wasn't hard.

Eventually, I was able to cajole the branch into bringing forth a handful of tiny pink blossoms. The blooms were small and pink, perfect and delicate and desperately out of place among the fan-shaped Ginkgo leaves.

Daylight filtered down through the boughs as I walked home after the lesson. The forest was beautiful. Since it was early autumn, the yellow of the leaves was fresh; the preservation upon them—the first of several before the season would be up—still glistening as it sank in. I was marveling at the yellow carpet, enraptured as always, when I was bowled over, and fell in a mess of limbs. There, half on top of me, I saw a young woman with gentle features and elbow-length red braids. She was wide-eyed and startled, and unfamiliar to me, but the red maple leaves pressed—almost painted—on the backs of her hands marked her as a Speaker of

Maple. I myself had a pair of yellow ginkgo leaves clinging to the hollows of my collar bones.

"Sorry! I'm so sorry," I said, extricating myself from underneath her and standing back up.

"Yes, I'm fine, thank you, um..." she paused for a moment and rose to her feet. "I was distracted. I should be the sorry one."

"Where are you headed?" I asked. I noted how the deep red of her dress stood out in the carpet of soft gold.

"I was hoping to find the Ginkgowood's Speakers. I'm from the Maple neighborwood, and I think we need help. Hopefully of a sort that the Ginkgo Speakers can provide." Her voice wavered as she talked, a pleading evident in her words. She looked exhausted. I reached out my hand. She took it and squeezed my fingers.

"I'm only a novice Speaker, but I can bring you to my teacher," I told her, pulling down the collar of my shirt to show her the leaves there. She let out a small sigh of relief and let me begin leading her back along the path I'd just come down.

The branches overhead arched in deliberate patterns, Spoken maps that could lead you anywhere in the wood—should you know how to read them, or at least, how to ask the trees for help. The Maplewood girl followed me with wide eyes. Through hollows in the stands of trees I could see my neighbors working—cooking, mending, sewing, and gardening, all tucked into homes Spoken from the trees. We passed the home of another Speaker, but one I didn't know well enough to introduce to the Maplewood girl. His home was on the edge of a clearing, where the trees wouldn't be bothered by the heat and smoke of his—amazing—baking.

The branches overhead weren't yet bare, turning the air a golden yellow. Even the Maplewood Speaker seemed impressed with the gold all around her. My great-uncle August had been a trader between the woods, and he'd described the Maplewood as having a rich carpet of red and an ever-present sweet scent. Even growing up with that, the Maplewood Speaker seemed impressed by the Ginkgowood.

My mentor Amber lived deep in her tree, which had been Spoken into a gentle nest of a home many generations ago. Its trunk was wide and it seemed to fold into itself somewhere, where the sloping boughs met a twist in the trunk. I turned into the hollow space and followed gentle, worn-smooth, spiraling steps downward. The root ball had been spread out and shaped with Speaking until it formed a burrow; a home with kitchen, bedroom, common room, library, and pantry. I loved the warm glow of the place, the way the amber lamp roots had been Spoken into shelves and earth had been Spoken solid and smooth.

The Maplewood girl followed me closely. I always found the place a comfort, and I could tell that the girl was also settled some by the calm space. "Amber?" I called out.

"Bee?" The slight padding of footsteps floated into the room around her voice. Amber had been stocking the pantry, it seemed—her tree was female, granting her ample fruit without a single whisper. She wasn't one to waste this gift. She smiled a broad, true smile. "Bee! What brings you back so soon?" She had an apron on over her blouse, and her black hair was pulled into a bun—as it was only when doing housework. Her eyes flicked to the foreign

Speaker, and I saw in her eyes that the girl had caught her interest.

"Um, hello," the strange Speaker began. "I'm here on behalf of the Maplewood." She held up her hands. "We have a problem. The Maplewood has a bit of a shortage of Speakers—well, Novices really." Her fingers were intertwined, wringing with her words. "A shortage in that we have none." The words were heavy, hanging in the air like syrup.

"How long?" Amber asked.

"I was selected three cycles ago," the Speaker said. All the neighborwoods, I knew, tested for gifted children to train as Speakers at the same five-year interval. "Even then," she continued. "I was the only one. So, really the shortage has been since before that."

"Two complete cycles without any apprentices?" Amber frowned, and her eyes focused inward. "Ten...almost fifteen years of children, since there have been new novices?"

The Maplewood girl nodded. "I was tested young myself. I was only nine when I was accepted as a novice, because we've had so few truly gifted children born in our neighborwood," The Maplewood girl said, her brows knitted. "I'm scared for us."

That explained her age. I had been sixteen when I was tested for the Speaker's gift, and wouldn't become a full Speaker until the end of the cycle—just after my 21st birthday. Yet here she was, this Maplewood Speaker, a full Speaker of her wood, and she was maybe a year older than me.

"So, nearly twenty years," Amber said.

"Yes." The Maplewood Speaker pursed her lips. "We can't fix this on our own. If we knew what was causing us to lose our connection to the wood, we could reknit it; if we knew where the Speaking was going, we could try to cajole it back to our children. But that's not working. It's just...leaving." When she said those words, the Speaker seemed ready to cry.

After a moment of silence (save for the gentle crackling of the fire in the corner) Amber Spoke a soft suggestion of calm. Her words settled over us: a warm, soft blanket. The Maplewood Speaker's hard worry melted some, softening into a gentler concern.

"I can call the Ginkgowood Speakers together. We can discuss what is in our power to help the Maplewood," Amber said, her voice back to normal. "We have much to consider before we can offer our help to you, miss…?"

"Gia." What a lovely name.

Gia nodded at Amber. She must have known that the Speakers would want to talk together before offering help to her and her people, no matter how desperate the situation felt to her. I silently thanked Amber for having Spoken a comfort around us.

Amber pulled off her apron and turned to me. "Bee, would you please find someplace for the Speaker to stay?" It was my turn to nod.

"She can stay with me," I offered, smiling at the girl as she stood beside me.

As Amber began to mutter to herself and look for something, I guided Gia back up the stairs. She was quiet, and remained that way as I led her to my home.

The calm hung on our shoulders as we walked, giving the neighborwood an unspecifiable quality—almost dreamlike in its softness. It had been years since I'd had calm Spoken onto me. It was a common Speaking upon children, and one simple enough that most anyone could spin it in some fashion. Even so, it had been a long time. I'd forgotten how nice it was.

My home was a warm, open one, made from four trunks Spoken into arching walls enclosing a single room a dozen feet off the ground. I was halfway up the flattened branch stairs, which twisted and wound up to my front door, when I felt the calm slip away and the cool bite of the air return to my awareness.

Gia paused—she was also feeling the edge return to the world. I hesitated, watching her, concerned but hesitant to ask her how she was doing. But she quickened her pace once again, following me into the comfort of my small home. The wood had been Spoken smooth and worn soft. The branches of the four great Ginkgos that made my home wove a sturdy, solid basket of floor and ceiling.

I held open the heavy curtain over my home's front entrance for the Maplewood girl and saw her smile as she ducked inside. The room was wide and simple. My bedroll sat against one wall; several overstuffed pillows rested on the floor around a low table; and my large, full kitchen (with both a stove and a hearth!) took up nearly half of what was left unclaimed. I've always found it a kind and open place, and Gia seemed to find it a pleasant place to be. I fixed some tea, broth, and shortbread cookies. She was quiet.

Rain came to the Ginkgowood that night. It pittered down through the leaves, and I could feel the cool dampness of the air that always accompanies a soft drizzle. The rain picked up as the night wore on, the thrum upon the interlaced-branches overhead growing more insistent as the night grew deeper.

I slept lightly and little, rising early in the small hours of the morning. The Maplewood girl tossed as she slept, her mind no doubt wracked with worry for her wood. As I moved about the room, putting water on the fire and warming my toes, the Speaker stirred. I glanced over, afraid I'd disturbed her, but she didn't move again.

I set some acorn tea to steep, some honeyed beechnuts to roast on the hearth, and considered what to do for breakfast. I had plain leavened bread, but the Maplewood was far enough from the Ginkgowood that the trip took three days, even running intermittently. She wouldn't have had a hot meal in that time, so I figured I ought to give her one.

I tried to cook quietly, so as not to disturb her. She slept curled into herself, her arms tucked tight against her torso. Her hair had slipped out of its braids in her sleep, ringing her head with red. The spill of hair framed her face, softening the taut lines that spread across it. She woke only when the sun was spilling across the floor of my home, the leaves of the neighborwood tinting the dawn light with the richness of gold that had always been my favorite thing about that time of year.

Gia didn't wake slowly, but started up with a breathless gasp. Her legs were tangled in the blanket, causing her to twist up further in her anxiety. I dropped a pan of heavy biscuits onto the stove and hurried to her side, skidding and scraping across the ground as I came to my knees beside her.

"What-" she stammered. She rubbed at bleary eyes with the heels of her palms.

"You're in the Ginkgowood," I said, my voice as low as I could make it. She trembled, her ankles still twisted up. I reached out a hand gingerly, offering her what comfort I could. "You're safe. The Speakers of Ginkgo are discussing how to help the Maplewood." My words were hushed, as soothing as I could make them without slipping into Speaking.

My guest blinked the sleep from her eyes and looked at me. Her eyes were so wide that I thought she might begin to cry. But she just nodded, reaching out to take my hand. She held onto me and took a deep breath, her eyes closing again as she settled herself. As she breathed, her chest rising and falling in rhythm, I wondered what it must be like in the Maplewood for her to be consumed by such deep and desperate fear.

"I presume you've no word," Gia said flatly after a handful of long moments.

"Nothing yet, no." She nodded, unsurprised yet still disappointed. I patted her hand and waved toward my kitchen. "Let's eat." Her grip on me tightened as we rose to our feet, but she let me go, settling for following close as I walked over to the stove.

I'd gathered the beechnuts to cool in a bowl, steeped the morning tea, cooked a small pot of hot cereal, and baked two sweet palm-loaves. My tree was filled with the smell of hot grains and honey. To top it all off, I retrieved a small jar of blackberry jam from the back of my top shelf. I had several of the small jars, as my mother was fond of making the sweet preserves during the summer berry season, and I was particularly glad to have something for my weary guest. I handed Gia one of the bowls and offered her the jam. I took my own bowl and walked over to the low table in the corner, scooting past her to pull over a pair of sitting cushions.

She sat down in one fluid motion, folding her legs up underneath herself. She put her bowl down across from mine as she settled, but then just stared into it. I waited for her to start, but she didn't.

"Um, Miss?" Her face stayed blank. "Gia?" I repeated. She blinked and looked up at me, eyes glassy.

"Sorry," she said, a waver in her voice. "What?"

I nodded. "Gia. You need to eat. You're exhausted." She nodded, and slowly moved to pick up her spoon and start to eat. I watched her as subtly as I could while eating my own breakfast. Though it was more indulgent than my typical breakfast, she seemed to enjoy the sweet roll with blackberry jam. I was proud of my cooking.

She scraped insistently at the bottom of her bowl and I could tell that I was right — she had really needed to eat. When she finally set the spoon down, apparently satisfied that she'd gleaned all that she could, I rose. I took both of our bowls over to the stove. I set mine on the counter, but spooned some more cereal into hers. I brought Gia a new cup of tea along with her bowl, and told her that I was going to fetch more water. She nodded, blowing gently on her drink.

And so I descended from my cabin with a large wooden bucket in hand into the early morning fog of the Ginkgowood. The mist was cool on my skin and I couldn't help but smile as I walked. The neighborwood looked particularly soft in the morning light; the haze of fog smoothing all the wood's edges. I walked barefoot, enjoying the dampness of the leaves. I left my bucket by a small creek and continued on to Amber's home. Guilt nagged at me, telling me I should've been honest with Gia, but I shook it as best I could. There had been no need to worry her further.

"Amber?" My voice was barely above a whisper. I cleared my throat. "Amber?" I called out, loud enough this time.

"Bee? I'm in the pantry," she said from somewhere off the main room. I followed the sound to find her on her tip-toes, reaching towards the back of her highest shelf. "Morning. I hope your walk was peaceful." I nodded.

"I was wondering—how did it go yesterday?" I wrung my hands, my fingers twisted up as my thumb worried my palm. "Gia—Gia—she's distraught. I'm worried for her."

Amber rocked back onto her heels. "As a Speaker, your work is to care for the Ginkgowood. You'll be asked to enrich and care for the wood, and to be a helpful and engaged member of our neighborwood. You'll sing to the skies to soften the weather, and ask the bushes for bushels of berries." This much I knew. The neighborwood would wither without our care. "We are not, however, asked often to make decisions. Our actions are subtle ones. We talk to the wood, we talk to each other, but we never really talk to others' woods." Amber paused, her face taut. "This isn't really something that has happened before. As such, we don't have any solutions yet." I nodded an acknowledgement. "The Speaker looked rather unwell yesterday, so I think we'll try to come up with a solution before we involve her in the discussion."

I knew I didn't have much time before Gia would begin to wonder. "Thank you, Amber." She nodded. "Please, let me know what the Speakers are saying."

Amber reached out her hand to me, patting me on the arm. "We'll do what we can."

With that, I left. The morning was already light, effusing the wood with a gentle glow as the light met with the last of the morning mist. I jogged back to the stream and filled the bucket. It was heavy enough that I had to slow my pace to keep from sloshing water down my front.

The morning mist had disappeared by the time I made it home. The day was warming up. When I got to the top of the stairs at last, water bucket in hand, I found that Gia was sitting exactly where I'd left her.

I could tell she'd moved; the cup in her hands was steaming, so she must have refilled it. But her feet were folded in that particular way, and her back was slumped just the same.

"Gia, I'm back," I said as I walked in, not wanting to startle her.

"Hello, Miss." She said without raising her head.

"Oh, please-"

"Bee, right?" She looked at me. Her eyes were watery, her face pale, but even so, she had an earnestness to her.

"Yes." I put the bucket down just inside the door. "Yeah, it's Bee." She smiled, but her smile was weak, watered down like sunlight through rainclouds - a visible effort, but hardly half the effect.

"Welcome back."

I wondered what it was about her that compelled me to fuss over her as if she were completely helpless. After all, she was a full and proper Speaker, while I was still a novice. I hesitated, standing near her for another moment before returning to the counter, to scrub up after breakfast.

Gia sat at the table. I watched her out of the corner of my eye, careful not to stare. I continued cleaning, and noticed for the first time that she didn't have a bag. A three-day walk would've required... something. But no, there she was with only the clothes on her back.

"Gia," I asked. "Why don't you have anything with you?"

"Huh? Oh," she pursed her lips and tucked a braid behind her ear before continuing. "I put what I needed in my pockets."

"Three days of rations in a pocket?" I raised my eyebrow.

"I took bread and a canteen. It was all I needed."

"Well, where's the canteen?"

She shrugged. "I dropped it when it was empty. It was awkward to hold while I ran."

Her frailty suddenly made sense—her pale face; her exhaustion; her distraction. I fetched another cup of water and sat beside her.

"Why did you run? Fifteen years without new novices, but now you run full tilt to a neighboring wood," I asked.

"Something snapped in me," she said. "There are enough of us for now, enough Speakers. Everyone is nervous, but they're not terrified. But after a second cycle without any apprentices, I realized… I realized that if something doesn't change, we'll all be gone without realizing it."

I didn't say anything more to that, just handed her the water. I didn't know what to say, so I just watched her. Her braids were loose, thin wisps escaping them. She was pale (quite unlike myself) but on top of that her fingers felt clammy. She was sick with worry, that much was clear.

Without any better idea of what to do, I put my arm around her. For a half-second, she stiffened, her whole body tensing up as she whipped her head around at me, eyes wide. But just as fast, she softened and shifted her weight towards me.

"Thank you," she whispered, so softly that I wasn't sure if she even intended for me to hear her. I patted her arm.

"The Maplewood'll be alright," I said after another long stretch. Gia turned her head into my shoulder at this, something leaving her at the mention of her home. I almost regretted saying anything, but she wrapped her arms around me and I could feel her shuddering. Heat spread across one shoulder, and I held her as she cried.

We sat like that for hours; until the sun was down and Gia was out of tears. When I started to move away, ready to roll out the sleeping mats, she took hold of my sleeve and followed closely. I could feel her nails through my shirt.

She held my arm when we went to sleep, clutching me like I was the last thing between her and nightmares. I figured that was probably the truth, and lay as still as I could.

The nest two days passed with agonizing slowness.

On the morning after I visited her, Amber came by my home with a nutty spread and assurances that yes, she would let me know when the Speakers had made a decision, and to stop worrying. This left Gia and I to discover that neither of us was the particularly patient sort.

I tried to distract Gia (and, to be fair, myself) during that time. I spent hours cooking complicated meals, with recipes I'd learned from my mother. I showed Gia the neighborwood, pointing out where Speaker May's partner was weaving blankets for their future child; where my mother lived; and where the Ginkgowood held market days. I even spent hours relaying to her all of the stories that I had been told as a child about the nature of the Ginkgowood. I learned quickly that the stories that were told in the Maplewood were quite different, even when they were the same—in the Maplewood, Rabbit in "The Sparrow and the Rabbit" isn't a baker, but a syrup maker, and Sparrow's wings are red, not gold.

The moments in between, when the air between us filled with anxiety, I would assure Gia that the Ginkgowood would not let her people down.

On the morning of the third day though, one of the other novices showed up at my door.

"Bee! Bee, get up!"

"Aiden?" I swept aside the curtain to see him there. His face was flushed and his breath caught in his throat. He was clearly in a hurry, though I wasn't sure why.

"The Speakers want us! They're meeting and they want us too!"

I glanced over my shoulder. Gia sat at the table, a curious expression on her face as our eyes met. I turned back to Aiden, a twisting in my gut.

"Did Amber say-"

"You can't bring the Maplewood Speaker." So Amber had known I'd ask. I was glad, then, that she'd sent Aiden. He let expressions and tones of voice slip past him, and I could feel my brow furrowing as I thought. He wouldn't read anything into my face. Why would Amber ask for me to leave Gia alone? She was a stranger here, and a stranger lost in her own despair. She needed company. Aiden's words broke my reverie. "Bee, come on, let's go."

"One moment," I said, turning to Gia. She looked much better than she had three days ago. She'd re-braided her hair — braids ringed her head, pinned tightly into place. The color had returned to her face and the focus to her eyes. "Um—"

"I heard," she said. I hesitated, waiting for her to continue. She didn't. So I turned about and followed Aiden away from my home. Away from Gia.

We walked quickly and wordlessly. Aiden was breathless with excitement over the prospect of making decisions with the Speakers. I was concerned for Gia.

The neighborwood was still dark, a tinge of watery pink in the sky the only indication of the coming dawn. We wound through the trees toward a large clearing where everyone in the wood could gather. It was full of people — novices and Speakers and neighbors alike. At the sight of all the people, Aiden visibly deflated.

When all of the Speakers and novices were present, the oldest Speaker—a wizened old man named Faa—stood. His golden robe seemed to dwarf him and his white hair rebelled against gravity, but his eyes had yet to cloud with age. As he stood, the clearing went quiet.

"Good morning, all," Faa said. "The Maplewood is in trouble. For some unknown reason, the Maplewood has no new Speakers, no new Novices. They are running out of Speakers." A murmur rippled through the neighbors, and Faa waited for it to fall away before continuing. "For the past three days, we Speakers have considered how to help. At last, we have an idea to present to the neighborwood." He turned and returned to his seat. Another Speaker, Tanner, stood and came forward. He was a sturdily built man, with a voice that carried over the assembled with little effort.

He cleared his throat and took a deep breath before beginning. "We have decided that—if the neighborwood finds it acceptable, of course—we'll send some of our Speakers to the Maplewood on a rotation. We'll start with six-week rotations of three Speakers each. We'd also evaluate the effectiveness of the six-week rotation after several months, of course. When the Maplewood starts to have new Speakers again, we'll leave." Many of the Speakers nodded at this, sitting straight and watching the neighbors. The others tried to mask their malcontent, but I could see a handful shifting where they sat.

"Is that all?" I asked, rather loudly. I hadn't meant to open my mouth, let alone practically shout at a Speaker, but the solution that he offered seemed a pittance.

Tanner frowned at me. "Do you have a problem with helping our neighbors, novice?"

I rose to my feet, shifted the collar of my shirt to show the leaves which noted my status as a novice Speaker, and began talking. "The Maplewood has waited two cycles. In that time, they haven't had a single Novice. Even the cycle before that, they only had one, a novice accepted to the order of Speakers at just nine years old." The neighbors around me muttered to one another, an air of concern and confusion echoing through them. "The Speaker who came to us was that child. She's sick with worry for her people. We can't sit here and let things get worse."

"We aren't letting it get worse," Tanner snapped back at me. "We're helping them. We're giving what we have to give—our time, and our skills. What more is there to give?"

"It's not enough!" I said. "Your solution is to wait and, what, hope that eventually things will get better on their own?"

"What do you propose?" Tanner asked. I frowned. I didn't have any other solutions, but I knew that this wasn't enough. He responded to my hesitation with a haughty eyebrow. "You criticize our solution without offering one of your own? Why should we, who have decided to help people whom we owe nothing, have to listen to a girl who can't even try to think of a better way to help?"

His words lit a fire in my gut. I'd spent the past three days fostering Gia, a gentle, broken soul. Yet he dared insinuate that I wasn't putting effort into this? I could see Amber sitting with the Speakers; she bit her lip as Tanner talked.

"It took you three days to come up with your solution." I replied. "Three days that I spent caring for the ill woman who came to us for help. She ran here from the Maplewood, desperate for help." The neighborwood was usually a place of calm, of civility. I'd never lost my temper like this before, but it felt natural, the words insistent that I say them. My neighbors all seemed to frown as one.

Amber and Faa both rose, separately, but together. Amber stepped over several folks to stand by my side. I could feel her concern for me reaching across the space remaining between us. Faa touched Tanner on the shoulder, murmured something to him, and turned to the assembly. "Novice Speaker Bee has a point, my friends. We open our ears to you, to all the neighbors. We'll reconvene tomorrow morning to discuss alternative, or additional, longer-term solutions."

As folks started to leave, Amber patted my arm. "I think you could use a rest," she said, leaning towards my ear and talking low. I frowned at her. "Faa was right, you were compelling. You're compelling, I think, because you've taken on the Maplewood Speaker-"

"Gia," I interjected. Amber nodded.

"Because you've taken on Gia's burden. That's quite a task, and I know it's exhausting. You need a break."

She walked me back to her home and sat me down at the table. In front of me, Amber placed a cup of mead, a thick stew, and a small glazed roll. She sat down with a cup of tea for herself, and waited for me to eat. When I finished, she insisted on a lesson in Speaking.

"It'll distract you, get your mind off all this," she insisted.

"But what about—"

"I'll ask Aiden to go check on her, alright?" she said.

I relented.

I followed her through the neighborwood to a stand of trees that wanted for care. Brambles crept up around their trunks, curling outward, abutting the path. I sat on the path and cradled a vine, careful not to prick myself. I whispered to it, wheedling the needles dull. Vine by vine, I Spoke away the brambles' defenses. It was early evening before I finished to Amber's satisfaction and she told me to, at last, go home.

When I walked in, Gia looked up from the fire. She was cooking—I could smell tea and roasting potatoes. Her face was red from the heat, and she had strapped on the apron that I always forgot to use. She'd re-braided her hair, woven it into a plait that feathered into nothingness at the small of her back. I'd learned that playing with her hair was a nervous habit of hers, so the complex layering of the braid told me more about her state of mind than her words would.

"Oh, you're back!" she said, a smile breaking across her face. "Do you have news?" At the sight of my face—with an expression I only registered was present from her reaction to it —she hung the ladle on the edge of the cast-iron pot and approached me. Her face held a hundred unasked questions. Instead, she cupped my cheek in her hand and forced me to look her in the eye. "Bee?"

"The Speakers had a plan," I whispered. "It wasn't enough. Isn't enough."

She stood there, her hand on my face. "I...we can make it work." She said, wearing a sad smile that was as soft as her words. "My people, we'll do our best, whatever it is." Her pain and worry for her people wracked her, but she was better than she had been. She held herself together.

"No, we're going to do better. I have until tomorrow to come up with a better solution." I sighed. If she hadn't held me there, I would have turned away and shaken my head. "All the Speakers in the Ginkgowood took three days to come up with, 'We visit from time to time and let them wait for a natural end to the problem.'" Three days reassuring Gia, wasted. Reassurance only helps, I thought bitterly, if everything ends up okay.

Gia pulled me into an embrace. I could feel her pain, and my whole being ached in sympathy. Amber was right, I had taken on Gia's pain. But I couldn't bring myself to mind, not then, while we each held the other up as we hurt in tandem, mourning the Maplewood.

I only let Gia go when I could hear the tea begin to boil. We ate, cleaned up, and then lay down for sleep, all in silence, though neither of us slept at first.

We lay close enough to feel one another's body heat. I didn't slip into sleep even as the hours slipped past. All I could do was think, searching for some solution to the plight of the Maplewood. I watched Gia slip into an uneasy sleep as I thought. Even tossing and turning, soft whimpers and moans rising from her, her warmth, her presence, comforted me. A palmful of hours before dawn, she started weeping in her sleep. I touched her on the arm, hoping to pull her out of the dream. She mumbled, shaken from the pain, and curled into me. My heart skipped a beat, but as Gia fell back into her dreams, I wrapped my arms around her and held her close. She smelled like sugar, and I wondered if the whole of the Maplewood smelled like syrup. The thought made me smile, my face buried in her hair. It was straight, unlike mine, and soft in a different way. She settled against me then, like she was seeking my warmth in her unconsciousness.

I whispered a Speaking of sweet dreams to her. I felt the warmth of my breath held against my face by her hair. I hadn't Spoken anything onto another person in ages, and the feeling of whispering to the core of Gia was so pure I had to hold my breath to keep from tightening my arms around her. There was a delight in Speaking to trees and brambles, of course, but they don't react quite the same way—it doesn't echo back. The thought that I had then was so abrupt that I squeezed her tightly without meaning to, causing her to stir.

"Bee?" she mumbled.

"Sorry," I replied. "Go back to sleep." She nodded and nodded off fast, thanks to the sweet dreams I'd Spoken for her.

With Gia curled against me and an idea in my mind, I fell fast asleep, dead to the world, if only for a few hours.

When we woke, we ate quietly, and then I led Gia to the great clearing in the neighborwood. It was filling up when we got there. We sat and waited for the meeting to begin. Gia didn't ask me if I'd found a solution, and I didn't offer to tell her that I had—I wasn't sure what she would think.

When the whole of the neighborwood had gathered, Faa stood. He gestured to me and asked if I had a suggestion for the Speakers. Gia and I rose together. I took a deep, shaky breath, and then explained.

"I'll give my Speaking to the Maplewood. All of it. They can have every drop," I said. I heard a number of gasps, and Gia's small hand snatched at my arm, trying to pull me to face her. But I continued. "Speaking is part of who we are, yes, but that fact is exactly what means this should be possible! What we Speak to is the essence of a being, and Speaking itself is part of our essence. It's natural, inherent—it should be possible to influence." I took a deep breath. "You can Speak the gift out of me and Gia can take it to the Maplewood." I turned and nodded at Speaker Tanner. "Until then, we may help them as you suggested, but after a cycle they will no longer need our aid." Gia tugged harder at my arm but I leaned away from her, countering her weight with my own.

The entire clearing was filled with silence. Stunned, confused silence.

"I mean," I said, continuing because I didn't know what else to do. "I'm just a novice, I can't even consistently grow an apple. It's not like my Speaking would be missed."

"No," Faa said. "Don't give yourself. You have so much time left, so much fire left in you." He smiled deeply at me. It was a smile that made me feel warm and full, really and truly proud of myself. He 6turned to Gia and took a long, shaking breath before letting out a long, shaking sigh. "You're right, logically, it should work. But if you have to take the power away from someone...you can have my Speaking. I've served the Ginkgowood so many years...this is what I have left to give."

After several long moments where the clearing was quiet but for the rustling of leaves, the keeper of records, a Speaker named Gianna, rose to her feet as well. "I have less than half a cycle before my apprentice becomes a full Speaker. When they are ready to take my place, I'll go and give my Speaking to the children of the

Maplewood." After she said her piece, she waved a reassuring hand to someone behind me. Turning, I saw that it was her apprentice, Speaker Conna. Their eyes were wide with shock, with anxiety. I looked away, embarrassed.

Three more of the senior-most Speakers offered their Speaking to the Maplewood. I stammered, not having intended others to give up themselves, but each talked of a life spent in service to the neighborwood. Their Speaking would not be missed, each insisted. One professed a desire to bake pastries, another touched her belly and explained the want to care for her future child with all of her hours.

I was dumbfounded, and sat quietly while the Speakers talked among themselves and decided to head out the next morning for the Maplewood. As the meeting ended, I found that Gia and I were holding one another's hands with a mutual vice grip that had caused my fingers to go numb.

"That was impressive," Amber said, weaving towards us through the crowd of chattering neighbors as I rubbed feeling back into my hand.

"Thanks," I said.

That afternoon, Gia, Amber, the four Speakers who'd offered their gifts most immediately, and I prepared for the long walk to the Maplewood. Blankets, water, food—everything that we needed, we folded and packed neatly into soft rucksacks. Unlike Gia, we took our time, readying ourselves before the three-day trip.

The next three days were too long for my feet, but too short for my heart. Gia and I walked the whole way with our fingers intertwined, and slept in one another's arms.

When we entered the Maplewood, it was like walking upon a river of fire. The leaves were all reds and deep oranges; the color was as rich as the gold of the Ginkgowood. I leaned over to whisper to Gia—

"Is this how you felt when you saw the Ginkgowood?"

She smiled. "Probably not."

As Gia led us between the wide trunks of maple trees, neighbors started to gather —it wasn't often that people moved between woods, and they watched us walk. She led us to a wide clearing and had us wait for her to bring the Maplewood Speakers.

The clearing seemed to be rather similar to the one in which Ginkgo Speakers had stood and offered their gifts. I looked around while we waited, intrigued by the beauty of the scarlet maple leaves.

It wasn't long until the clearing was filled with neighbors and Speakers. Gia wandered back towards us, standing just beside me. I heard a soft murmuring wash over the crowd, hushed whispers, then a number of sharp breaths.

Faa turned to me when one of the Maplewood Speakers looked to our small island of yellow in the sea of red, and nodded to us. "Novice, would you deliver my gift to the Maplewood? This was your idea, after all."

My breath caught in my throat, but I nodded. Gia guided me forward, her hand steady on my arm. Faa closed his eyes, a wide smile breaking across his face. "I'm looking forward to being just another man," he said to us. Gia and I exchanged glances. I put my hand out; she patted me on the back and took a step away.

Speaking the gift was like trying to control the flow of a stream with a bucket of water. I Spoke to Faa's essence, asking that which was the very core of him to please disentangle itself from its eternal harmony. His soul didn't give up Speaking eagerly, but slowly, my words found purchase. Faa smiled—it was a fake smile, the kind that is so perfect it seems as genuine as the smile of a child when they see the golden air of a morning in the Ginkgowood. I knew the truth, though. Faa's being was echoing, separating itself from the gift inside him with great reluctance. It was, after all, a part of him.

As I whispered to Faa's gift, I felt warmth spread across my palms. The whole of the Maplewood watched us in silence.

I felt the Speaking flow from Faa and come to rest solidly around me. It felt like a glove, like I had water swirling around my hands. Once I had pulled all of Faa's speaking out of him, I whispered to it, telling it to find purchase within the neighbors here, within their children, and felt the weight of it drip from my hands into the earth of the Maplewood. As I finished, I could feel it starting to seep into the water, into the plants: into the Neighborwood and its people.

When I finished, Faa opened his eyes. He straightened his back, as if a great weight had been lifted, and nodded first to me, then to Gia, then to the rest of the Maplewood.

The other Ginkgowood Speakers exchanged nervous smiles. Their expressions were tentative and excited, and I could feel what they were feeling—after what I'd just done. At the edge of the clearing, I saw a young child watching us, bobbing up and down on the balls of their feet, full of energy. A man dressed in a deep red, similar to that of Gia's clothes, squeezed the child's shoulder. His fingers caught the fabric of the child's shirt, twisting it up in five little swirls of shadow.

I caught Gia's eye—her face was higher than I'd remembered. It took me a moment to understand why: she'd been slumped down for the past four days. At length, she had straightened her back, a weight lifted. A smile came from somewhere deep within her, and from her, tears fell onto the carpet of scarlet below us.

See Mads Alvey's story "Upon the Fallen Leaves of the Gingko Tree" online at

Metaphorosis. If you liked it, leave a comment. Authors love that!
Remember to subscribe to our e-mail updates so you'll know when new stories are posted.

About the story

Many of my story ideas start with a single line—usually the first line in the final draft—which repeats over and over in my mind. "Upon the Fallen Leaves of the Ginkgo Tree" was one of these stories. When I began the story, my walk to school every day involved going through a neighborhood which was lined with ginkgo trees, and the first line of the story came to me while I was walking through the neighborhood in the fall—upon the leaves.

I'm also invested in the idea that fiction is the way in which we as people come to understand ourselves and our world, and that speculative fiction is particularly significant in this. Because of this, I tend towards stories which involve the world ending better than it started. Once I had the starting line of the story, I mulled over a variety of scenarios that would let me have a hopeful or positive ending, and ended up with a draft of the story that (very) loosely resembled the final product.

A question for the author

Q: Do you write with a particular audience in mind?

A: I often write with myself as the intended audience. There are a lot of things that I enjoy seeing in stories, and when I write, I try to hit all of those notes. I try to include people like me—queer folks, gender minority folks, disabled folks; themes and subjects I care about; and evoke images that matter to me, or appeal to my sense of aesthetics.

I do write with the intent of sharing my work, but it matters to me that I, at the very least, start with a base that is true, first and foremost, to what I want in a story.

About the author

Mads Alvey lives in Lexington, Kentucky and is a full-time student at the University of Kentucky, seeking a degree in English. She plans to seek an MLS when she graduates, and settle down surrounded by books. When he has it, he splits his free time between crafting; cooking; gardening; amateur taxidermy; writing science fiction, fantasy, and satire; spending way too much time on the internet, and doting on his three rats.

malveyauthor.com, @ProperPuns

Just a Fire

A. Martine

by Addison Black, JAN. 3rd, 3075

Over the past year, we at MAELSTROM have covered stories which have often bordered on the sensational, such as the famous rivalry between siblings Amaterasu and Susanoo, the Japanese gods of the Sun and the Storms respectively. We have also notably touched upon the scandalous account of the giant Paul Bunyan's alleged affair with the Titan Selene. All of these have served a similar aim: to bring awareness of Lorendi, sanctuary of forgotten gods and goddesses, and bridge the gap keeping Humans and Lorendians separate.

In the midst of the cacophony of entities roaming Lorendi, it is often easy to forget some of the lesser-known, but no less interesting events. One such story is that of the Fall of Asgard, which many have attributed to the ongoing feud between former Valkyrie Brünnhilde and her father, the great Wotan.

It is common knowledge that all the inhabitants of Lorendi were forced to coexist after the collapse of their respective homes. It may be of interest for our readers to note that no one knows how Lorendi came to be. As more and more entities began to lose their homes, they found themselves inexplicably drawn to this vast and strange land, and found that they grew stronger within its borders. In this sense, Asgard is an anomaly; it appears to be the only place where the collapse was not instigated by humans, but the details of the episode remain unclear and contradictory.

Most of us have, at some point of our existences, idolized controversial figures, those insubordinate figureheads of change and defiance; for me, it has always been Brünnhilde, the powerful, enigmatic woman who lived and would have died for her ideals. The opportunity to decipher her story, essentially, is my childhood coming full circle.

According to the all but forgotten legend, after Brünnhilde's lover and nephew Siegfried was killed by Hagen, son of the dwarf Alberich, the erstwhile Valkyrie threw herself into his funeral pyre, maddened with her grief. The same pyre became a full-blown wildfire which consumed Valhalla and all the gods present, marking the grim end of this mythology. But in reality, only Siegfried, who had already perished, was a casualty that day; the hall was destroyed in the fire and spread throughout the whole of Asgard, robbing the gods and goddesses of their dwelling place — but they did not die with it.

It was not long before the protagonists of the Norse mythology dispersed throughout Lorendi. In the diverse landscape of this city, most of the former residents of Valhalla are not as noteworthy as those of other tales; indeed, when one has to contend with the unrestrained antics of the Greek pantheon or the staggering number of parties thrown by the Yoruba gods and goddesses, it is easy to lose sight of the Norsemen and women of Asgard. Doubtless because of the calamitous end of their cycle, they have retreated into more tranquil existences and successfully blended in with the other Lorendians, to a fault.

Thus, shedding light on the series of events that led to the catastrophic and fiery confrontation (often referred to as the Pyre Incident or Brünnhilde's Really Big Blunder) entails delving deeply into the relationship dynamics of some key characters of this episode.

Our investigation begins in the fields of Tarragon, a region in Southern Lorendi where those seeking respite from the sometimes hectic lifestyle of Aster or Amaryllis come to disengage. Eir, one of Brünnhilde's sister Valkyries, has agreed to welcome me into her lavish country home. She has invited their sister Sigrün for the conversation. Here in Lorendi, it never snows nor rains (due to an agreement between the many gods and goddesses of the weather), so the afternoon is mild and pleasant when the three of us sit down around ginger pastries and warm tea.

I try not to let my wonderment show; I am in the presence of legends, after all, and these are women whose storied place in history would dwarf anyone's confidence. Despite the fierce reputation they garnered when their exploits were recounted centuries ago, the Valkyries before me are even-tempered women who prefer walks in the sunny fields of Tarragon, these days, to bloody frays.

"Oh, believe me," Sigrün quips with a devilish smile, "we still engage in the occasional skirmish, but when your primary function has been obsolete for quite some time, it leaves more opportunity to unwind, which was frankly overdue."

I ask the sisters about their professional affiliation with their father Wotan, but the subject inevitably turns personal. Eir, who sees her sister Brünnhilde very often but has not spoken with their father in eons, tells me that while the Pyre Incident brought about the end of Asgard, it was a situation that had always been inevitable.

"I think," she tells me with a hint of displeasure, "that the whole affair was handled quite poorly."

Judging from Sigrün's weary expression, this is a conversation the sisters have often had.

Eir shrugs, implacable. "I do. Be fair, Sigrün, you remember some of those occasions as well as I do." She turns to me. "Brünnhilde was punished unfairly and often, although she was, on numerous occasions, absolutely powerless over the situation. Big things, small things, it mattered little. You see, she was always more resourceful — Wotan would say reliable — than the rest of us, so she was always called upon. She was even in charge of negotiations between the Vanir and the giants at one point, which had nothing to do with her Valkyrie duties. When things went well, Wotan would be proud: but that also meant that when they did not, everything would be her fault." Whether Eir's passion stems from sisterly partiality, or from her true belief, it is touching to behold.

"I will admit to that," Sigrün concedes. "But I also remember warning Brünnhilde that she often involved herself in things she shouldn't. She could never say no, and I told her to be careful. Besides, most of the Valkyries were starting to be jealous of the excess attention Wotan was giving her — except for us, of course." The aside is for me.

"On some level, that is true," Eir counters, "but ultimately, what doomed her was her involvement in stratagems on a grander scale which could at any given moment threaten the future of Asgard. Brünnhilde became a scapegoat because she was standing in the eye of the storm. It's as simple as that."

She is, of course, referring to the fabled ring that Loge persuaded Wotan to offer the Frost-Giants instead of Wotan's wife's sister Freia (which the giants had initially agreed upon).

"I don't think a lot people are comfortable mentioning this," Eir says with a bitter laugh, "but we all know that it's Wotan's incessant quest for the cursed ring that is the real source of Asgard's downfall, not anything my sister may or may not have done."

Watching them speak so casually about mythic events we humans have feasted upon for centuries dazes me temporarily. For the first time since I sat down with the sisters, I feel like I have pawed at something beneath the surface of my understanding. Whatever the rest of the world may have made out of it, this is just a family squabble for them, no different from the wine glasses and petty insults humans toss over Thanksgiving dinner with estranged relatives.

Sigrün has kinder words for her father than her sister does. This is surprising, considering that a long time ago, her lover Helgi was killed with the help of none other than Wotan. A suggestion of indulgence flitting across her lovely face, she says: "I agree wholeheartedly, but to say that they were at the source of everything that happened is unfair. In the long term, I believe that this was bound to turn out the way it did because everyone became different where the ring was concerned. Even the best of us could become monsters. And besides," she adds with a chuckle, "when I see the other father figures of Lorendi, it puts our own situation in sharp perspective."

The next stop to this journey leads me to the bustling streets of Aster, where one finds the most thriving and diverse community of Lorendians. Bars and shops manned by Pangu (the Chinese god of the Heavens and the Earth), Anubis (embalmer and protector of the graves), or even Bigfoot attract thousands of loyal customers on a daily basis. Further in the northern part of the neighborhood, an amusement park managed by the Loch Ness Monster and the Lady of the Lake is a popular fixture for the children of Aster. You will not find many of the more lofty characters of mythology here, but it is a welcoming and vivacious change of pace from Tarragon.

It is here, in a restaurant called Johnny's Appleseed that Loge has agreed to meet with me. Sporting retro shades, his long braided silver hair slung over his shoulder, he strolls in an hour late, smoking an electronic cigarette despite the waiter's protestations. After very short — and might I add, rather standoffish — introductions, Loge quickly broaches the subject.

"If you ask me," he says, blowing smoke rings in my direction, "I think that everybody is exaggerating the whole affair. It was just a *fire*."

I ask him about the ring, and his involvement in the story, an involvement some might consider the starting point of it all.

"That's what I do. People come to me for help and I help them, by any means. Wotan and Fricka wanted a way out of the mess Freia was going to be in with the Frost-Giants, and I gave them that. If it all went haywire from that point on, find the right people to blame."

"But surely," I ask him, "your participation was more instrumental than that. Is it not true that you were the one Wotan came to every time a crisis needed an underhanded solution?"

What is more: Alberich's ring was reportedly stolen by Wotan with Loge's help, which — among the many ensuing collateral costs — resulted in Brünnhilde being stripped of her immortality by Wotan and confined behind a ring of fire on a mountaintop, of Loge's own design.

"You say "underhanded", I say "subtle"," he answers, downing a cocktail in the blink of an eye, "and indeed, the fire was my idea. I'm rather proud of it: Wotan was leaning towards a cage made of fiery ice, but he has no taste for the aesthetics. Once again, it's not personal. People ask for my help and I help them. I'm sorry that Brünnhilde is sore about the whole affair, but to say that I was at the heart of Asgard's Fall is a bit of an overstatement."

It suddenly becomes clear to me that the outcome of the strife involving Asgard may have been due to nothing more than likability. A popularity contest, one that the temperamental, unpredictable Brünnhilde was bound to lose, especially when facing off with an influential man like Loge. A question comes to me unplanned, then, but I don't yet ask it. Loge has already changed the subject.

He seems generally unruffled about his life at Lorendi, and even admits that he prefers it to the one he led in Asgard; this place seems to have somewhat dulled his legendary mischievousness, replacing it instead with offhanded insouciance. Tipping backwards on his chair, he laughs throatily.

"It's a riot. People here are carefree and they don't dwell on the past. There is much less pressure to perform your duties here than there was before. Look around you: there are five different gods and goddesses of the sun, twenty personifications of love and fertility. Tricksters abound, and heroes and heroines meet their matches on a daily basis."

Perhaps because I am slightly annoyed by him, or perhaps because my curiosity has been needled by his nonchalance, the question re-emerges, coming to my lips before I can make it tactful:

"Did you actually see Brünnhilde tip over the pyre that burned Asgard down? Did anyone?"

"Now... whatever do you mean by that?" he asks, almost teasingly, pulling on his cinnamon-spiced cigarette.

"Many people," I elaborate, noticing how attentive he has suddenly become, "have accepted that the fire may have been an act of childish retaliation. But it seems to me that Brünnhilde would be the last person to benefit from such large-scale sabotage. Unlike people who, for example, would want their involvement in less-than-noble endeavors burned away in the debacle. People looking for a fresh start."

"Do you mean to say," he replies with laughter in his voice, "that you believe she either didn't do it, or else was coaxed into it?"

It wouldn't be the first time that emotionally vulnerable people had been taken advantage of, I proffer. Additionally, the entire event seems antithetical to the motivations people tack onto Brünnhilde. She has not continued a campaign of vindictiveness; in fact, she lives apart from everyone else, has done so for the past few centuries.

"Well," he leans in close, almost serious, for the first time "you're assuming that because you didn't know her. "Black Sheep Ousted From Family For Daring To Defy Them". Better yet: "Tortured Soul Manipulated Into Large-Scale Act Of Vandalism"." He gestures across the air with an open palm. "It does sound good on paper, I'll admit."

We both laugh, although no joke has been uttered there. I am not done with the matter; but for the moment, I let the question lie on the table between us, knowing full well that I will find no admission or good-natured insight behind Loge's determined indifference. He is happier to look to the future, and so I let him swerve the conversation back to Lorendi, and to his previous assurance that this is where redemption should be looked for.

He reaffirms the idea as we part ways.

"I think we're better off here and I think that this," he makes a general gesture to indicate the whole of Lorendi "would have happened anyway."

In a rare moment of contemplation, he adds, mounting his motorcycle: "myths and mythologies, folklores and fairy tales. All of this could never last. It had to end, somehow. We at Asgard just happened to go out in a blaze of glory." His sudden introspection seems to catch him off guard, and by the time he revs his engine, the mask of practiced casualness is back.

Amaryllis is less frenzied than Aster, but no less delightful. By day, it is not only an upper-class residential area, but also where some of the most luxurious boutiques and opportunities for recreational activities are located. It is, however, after dark that Amaryllis truly comes to life. Nightclubs and bars frequented by Lorendi's elite entertain them until dawn, and it is not uncommon to witness weddings and other parties being celebrated with pomp and grandeur. Many of the warriors who were brought to Valhalla by the Valkyries can be found here, chatting up sprites and fairies, and cavorting with centaurs and leprechauns.

Hildr, one of Brünnhilde's fellow Valkyries, meets with me in Saraswati's Den, a trendy hotel bar owned by the goddess of the same name, and where the Valkyrie happens to reside. She is among those of her sisters who chose to adapt completely to her new life, which suits the grandiloquence (some say pretentiousness) she has often been associated with. She is often seen partying with Aphrodite and Metztli, the Aztec goddess of the Moon, when she is not hosting a popular biweekly talk show on socialite life in the 31st century.

I am on edge again, but in a way that differs from when I encountered Eir and Sigrün. Hildr barely looks corporeal. She is the incarnation of opulence, and as she enters the bar, almost every head turns in her direction: sheaths of white silk artfully wrapped around her tall frame complement her platinum blonde curtain of hair; she moves with the ease of one who knows she is in command. I can't help but think that she must have been quite a sight on her horse in the battlefield, so many centuries ago.

She joins me and greets me charmingly, although her welcome lacks the warmth I felt with her sisters. Despite her imposing arrival, Hildr is anything but ardent; she is not interested in passionate arguments or zealous debates. The more I talk with her, the more it becomes clear that she has never been a strong proponent of the theory that Brünnhilde is a victim, that the fire was an accident, nor that Wotan had any responsibility in the downfall of Asgard. Still, in her debonaire attitude I sense a steeliness that could easily become callousness in a different light, a steeliness she makes only a halfhearted effort to conceal.

"Things are the way they are. Everyone thinks that just because we came here when our home became uninhabitable, and not because humans forgot about us, we *need* to find a reason, an explanation, someone to blame," she drawls over the din of voices surrounding us.

The question I asked Loge emerges again, but I've had enough time to compose it more diplomatically.

"According to you, Brünnhilde is unequivocally responsible, then?"

"Oh, without a doubt. I was there. We were all there." She says this without a hint of skepticism. The rapidity with which Brünnhilde's alleged culpability was accepted as fact is shocking, considering how far-reaching its effects have been.

I frame my question differently: "Is this characteristic of the Brünnhilde you knew and liked?"

"It was just a *fire*," she sighs, echoing Loge's condescension almost to perfection. Then, leaning closer with a conspiratorial look, she whispers: "*I* think that Brünnhilde was bored, and decided that she wanted to be at the center of some sort of exciting melodrama. She's always been that way. I think she was trying to distract us all from the fact that she had committed incest with her nephew Siegfried."

"Could it be," I advance, "less about anger or retaliation than an expression of her desperation? Or perhaps an attempt to force a new beginning at Asgard, by purging it of its convoluted mess? If she is to blame, that is."

"And kill us all in the process?" Hildr titters. "You are kind, but that theory is nonsense."

I know that I am toeing the line between journalistic integrity and the inexplicable inclination to defend a childhood hero, but I also recognize that there is no love lost between Hildr and Brünnhilde. She might be as biased as I am, no matter how much she feigns apathy in the matter. I begin to wonder whether a specific incident is to blame, but think better of asking her. I have a suspicion that Hildr's graciousness is mostly skin deep.

When asked about her opinion on the Human-Lorendian relationship and whether the gods' lives in Lorendi are a fitting substitute for their respective places of origin, Hildr is lost in thought for a long moment.

"At the risk of sounding complacent, I think that the lives we lead here are truly unparalleled. We're all birds of a feather, to borrow your Earthly expression."

"That might surprise our readers. It is widely assumed that most of you must be homesick."

"Of course it's assumed," she smiles in patronizing amusement, leaning back in her chair, "but I don't believe we ever needed humans worshipping us to survive; if that was the case, even Lorendi couldn't save us. We would have faded into oblivion eons ago."

"Why agree to tell your version of events to MAELSTROM's readers, if you Lorendians are self-sufficient?"

"Because our stories matter," Hildr replies, as if this were the most obvious answer in the world, "and they would have mattered whether there were people to tell them to or not. Together, we are stronger and more complex than we were separated. Ask anyone of any other mythology here, and they will tell you the same stories: betrayals, incest, illegitimate children, murder, jealousy... Brünnhilde, Wotan, Siegfried, and the ring? It was nothing special, by any standard, so I suggest we stop thinking it was."

She waves her hand loftily as she says this, as if to brush a ridiculous notion away. Slicing through the roasted peach pie she ordered, Hildr continues: "*combine* these stories and make them interact, however, and you suddenly find yourself with a riveting spectacle. Lorendi is like a micro-universe that gathers all the tales and allegories of the world, as it was meant to be. We represent all of History, in its oddity and its diversity. We reflect the changing mentalities of humans and their cultures over the millennia, and if there is anything your readers should retain, it's this: we are special."

As we part, Hildr turns to me again, and I can see that indifference has crept back into her expression.

"I don't go around saying this often, because some people still feel raw about the debacle, but I don't regret any of it. I think the fire did us all a favor." The elevator doors close on her as she looks down at her communication device, her attention already elsewhere.

Fricka has declined to speak to MAELSTROM for this story, but surprisingly, Wotan has agreed give us his perspective on the narrative. The man himself, former Supreme Ruler of Asgard. I try to contain my excitement, lest it render me unfocused. In order to meet him, I travel to Angrec, on the West Coast of Lorendi, where many financial and political institutions have settled themselves. The older, more established gods, goddesses, and beings often purchase grandiose estates here, and its seaside location makes it a perfect place to take short but sweet vacations.

Wotan co-owns many of these residences along with Zeus and Anansi, and has made his fortune leasing them to the entities who flock to their shores, looking for more upscale lifestyles. I arrive in his opulent home and I am seated on a beautiful sunbathed patio by one of his assistants and offered a drink. As I wait, I become rather nervous, expecting, from the many stories and accounts surrounding him, a boisterous and roguish man. He is anything but. The man I meet is courteous and pleasant, and there is no trace of arrogance in his stance. Waves of fiery red hair fall loosely over his shoulders; in fact, everything about him seems loose and deliberate. Unlike his brother Loge, he removes his sunglasses when he speaks to me, despite the fact that we are outdoors. It is hard to believe that this is the selfsame person who has committed adultery innumerable times and betrayed his closest relatives in his relentless pursuit for Alberich's ring. Still, I keep my guard up. I have interviewed too many a charming entity not to know better.

I ask him about his role in the Fall of Asgard and, after a careful pause, the god launches into a leisurely diatribe. Watching him speak is simply enthralling; it doesn't take long for me to understand why everyone is drawn to this articulate and persuasive man, in spite of the fact that half of what he says seems wholly calculated and insincere.

I notice, as he speaks, that he never once acknowledges his purported obsession with the ring, nor does he mention Brünnhilde. I decide to be blunt.

"Did you see her do it, and if so, do you think it was intentional?"

Wotan deflects my first question so masterfully that I almost don't catch it; instead, he leans into the latter part.

"Ah, Brünnhilde." He chuckles warmly, as if thinking fondly of a petulant, rebellious child. "That girl has always had a viselike hold on me. I hear that she's been going around accusing me of having ruined her life. I think she needs a scapegoat because everyone seems to blame her for having spread the fire that destroyed Valhalla. But that's all it was, just a fire."

Unlike with the others, when Wotan says this, the Pyre Incident seems indeed reduced to a minor skirmish, something small, something not worth bothering about. Intentions and motivations barely seem to register for him.

He continues: "It was an accident, all those who were there know that, but if a little gossip and rumors are that bothersome to her, she can keep lambasting me if she wants. I think that she will find that whether they were initially angry about losing their home or not, most inhabitants of Asgard will agree that Lorendi has been very kind to them. She can get out of her self-imposed exile whenever she wants."

"But what about the many incidents before that? What about the one involving Siegfried, for example? Surely Brünnhilde has reasons to be angry not only with you, but with all the men who have wronged her in her life." I would be angry too, if I had a father like him, I almost say to illustrate my point; but I think better of it.

"Everyone thinks her punishment was unwarranted. The truth is, I was never ungrateful for the consideration she always showed me; but you see, I am a ruler. I must not appear fickle, volatile; I must appear to be a man of my word, one who does not condone trespass and defiance. When I decided to leave her on the mountain and strip her of her immortality, it was for her own protection. I was doing her a favor. The ring of fire was entirely my idea, I'm rather proud of it. Loge was partial to a cage made of burning ice, but I've always been more creative than him when it comes to this," he adds with twinkle in his eye (it is now unclear whether the ring of fire should be credited to Loge or to Wotan).

Despite his placid facade, I can see that Wotan is tired of speaking about this chapter of his life, and especially about his daughter. Nevertheless, as much as I would rather avoid irritating him, this is the main reason this investigation was launched, and it is the key to understanding why Valhalla imploded in such a spectacular fashion. More so than Hildr or Loge, Wotan's detachment pricks in a particularly painful way. He is, after all, Brünnhilde's own father, but seemingly the one least concerned about her fate. So I push him further about his theories regarding the Really Big Blunder.

"In the confusion of the brawl, anyone could have been responsible. Anyone, in fact, could have done such a thing, for very different reasons. Asgard had many enemies, some of whom have been said to include Loge," I tentatively proffer.

When he answers, he disregards the question underneath my question.

"I think that there are long-term causes and short-term causes. If we only focus on the short term, then it appears that I am the instigator and that Brünnhilde was a victim. If you want my opinion, I think that she should have made better choices about the men she chose to surround herself with. I always thought that falling in love with Siegfried was not a good idea and the fact that he died in such a fashion is truly regrettable. Do I regret my actions, however? Absolutely not. In each situation, one must weigh the outcomes, and I always pick the outcome that will produce the least damaging results. No one comes out of battles completely unscathed and I would think she'd know that, what with being a Valkyrie and all."

He lets the words hang between us, then elaborates on the long-term reasons. I am amused to note that he shares an almost identical opinion with Hildr on this matter.

"I think that in this scope, Asgard is in no way different from any of the other Lorendi folks' homes. We all collapsed, albeit in different ways. Many of us Lorendians have had to deal with a millennium of grudges and small grievances, and you make a compelling point. If it had not been Brünnhilde accidentally tipping over the funeral pyre, it would have been Alberich instigating a riot, the Jötnar storming Asgard, or Freia and Thor getting into a heated argument that destroyed the sacred halls of our home. I think we tend to try rationalizing the Pyre Incident to the point of obsessing over the details when one should be looking at the greater picture. I think our time was bound to come to an end, and this is something I've always accepted. It's the only reason why I have found it so easy to forgive and forget, and I wish Brünnhilde would do the same."

Brünnhilde has refused to sit down with us for an interview, thus depriving us of the most valuable point of view in this whole story. I suspect that she is handling too much grief over the death of her lover Siegfried, among other vitriol, and if Wotan is telling the truth, the guilt of having burned down Asgard by accident must surely weigh on her deeply. Perhaps with time, she will be able to bring herself to a point of closure, but for the time being, we are left with an almost — but alas, not wholly — complete story.

"Is there anything you would like to tell your daughter, in case she reads this article?"

Initially, Wotan dismisses the idea. Not for the first time during this investigation, I feel myself step out of my reporter's shoes, and stand as a woman, asking for another woman's sake. After a few moments where he seems to be deciding something, Wotan softens. He turns his stare to the distance where the sunsets are dyeing the clouds in gradient hues of scarlet. For a very long time, he squints into one of Lorendi's many setting suns before finally turning to me again.

"I do, actually. At some point I realized, since I've been living here, that what I used to think was important really isn't, you know? I thought, before in Asgard, that once you lost love it was over. I thought that once you were provoked, nothing mattered but getting justice for the offense. I thought that the unshakable pursuit of a goal outweighed everything else. Lorendi truly puts everything in perspective. Even the ring, which invaded my every thought, is lost, never to be found again. I heard they turned the whole thing into a popular book series a few centuries ago, *The King of the Rings* or something," he nods wisely. "Even if we never see each other again, I suppose I want her to find it in herself to realize the same. Only then can one truly start over."

Brünnhilde lives in Valeria, where most of the demigods, demigoddesses, and lesser folklore entities, as well as many of the smaller animals of the myths and folklores reside. It is rather separate from the rest of Lorendi, more so than Tarragon, but I am told that it is a pleasant place to live. Our readers might remember Valeria from a story covered by one of my fellow journalists, in the fourth issue of Mores and Icons, concerning the successful activewear business venture launched by Br'er Rabbit and his Senegalese cousin Leuk, the cunning hare.

Through the many collected instances surrounding the shunned Valkyrie, a patchwork has emerged. I simultaneously feel like I know Brünnhilde, and don't know her at all: she is a sad, lonely, possibly confused woman, but she also remains a mystery.

I would have relished a chance to hear her own words. Brünnhilde may have refused our invitation because she thought that her character would be assassinated. But perhaps she would have appreciated knowing that among us mortals, she continues to be celebrated for her singularity, no matter her part in Asgard's Fall. It is regrettable that her voice is glaringly absent in the panorama, and no amount of my personal of professional investment will be enough to change that fact.

However, while we may not have gathered her side of the tale, a bigger picture, is discernible. We may never know more than what was revealed in bygone and sometimes contrasting accounts of the entities who were involved in the incident, but it is clear that many, if not all of them (save Brünnhilde, perhaps) have moved on from it. The Lorendians have, for the most part, chosen to embrace their new homes and coexist peacefully, putting the rickety past behind them.

One must conclude that many of these characters, as Wotan and Hildr have so eloquently said, live similar lives and often meet similar ends, and the details don't matter. The exchange between all of these tales and events has produced a world that continues to fascinate humans of the 31st century, a world which will hopefully encourage them to tap into the mythological histories just waiting to be happened upon. Simultaneously, however, the more stories we publish, the more I hope our readers come to realize that these entities are not so different from us after all: young women still hate their fathers sometimes, unrequited love abounds, and egos can govern many a relationship.

It's a disappointment, and it's a relief.

A disappointment for the little girl in me who saw Brünnhilde as the epitome of uncompromising strength: ultimately, she is as flawed, if not more, than I thought her to be.

A relief for the woman I am today, precisely for those same reasons: I can gently remove her from her pedestal, and with it, the unattainable expectations I had held myself to, as I tried to emulate her.

Short of doing away with our heroes altogether, we can at least try to forgive them, even if we are no closer to understanding them.

Next month, we delve into the legendary rivalry between Ra and Apollo, the respective Egyptian and Greek gods of the Sun, and the confrontation that nearly robbed Lorendi of sunlight for a century.

See A. Martine's story "Just a Fire" online at Metaphorosis.
If you liked it, leave a comment. Authors love that!
Remember to subscribe to our e-mail updates so you'll know when new stories are posted.

About the story

"Just a Fire" was initially inspired by a lifelong love of fairy tales and mythologies from around the world; their occasional absurdity triggered in me a strong interest in retellings and parodies. More specifically, it was the manner in which stories across time and cultures resembled each other that I always found compelling, and I've always wanted to feature that in one of my tales.

As I began to write "Just a Fire", however, I found myself drawn to another aspect of storytelling: the notion of subjective truths and bendable perceptions. At its core, more so than a take on a portion of Norse mythology, this is about the way miscommunications and grudges (petty and profound) can divide people on the notion of what they know and believe to be fact.

"Just A Fire" is the first of many stories I set in the fictional country of Lorendi, each of the pieces detailing how famous fairy tale and mythology incidents have impacted their respective characters, often in the form of conflict involving unreliable points of view, rumors and damaging word-of-mouth.

A question for the author

Q: What are you reading now?

A: At the moment, I am juggling between:

- *Anne Sexton's Complete Poems* (Anne Sexton)
- *We Need to Talk About Kevin* (Lionel Shriver)
- *Little Fires Everywhere* (Celeste Ng)
- *In the Night Garden* (Catherynne M. Valente)

About the author

Aïcha Martine Thiam is a poet, writer, musician and artist who writes in English and in French, two of her native languages. She travelled the world as a child, and studied at the University of Montréal and Columbia College Chicago. Home is wherever the sea is near.

www.maelllstrom.com, @Maelllstrom

All the Colors I Cannot See

L'Erin Ogle

I remember everyone being lit up in colors when I was a little kid. They wore vivid blues and pinks and greens and yellows. Everyone dripped in thoughts and feelings. They were painted with sky blue happy or scarlet red mad, thunderhead gray sad and bright orange excited. I loved looking at everyone wearing their hearts out like that, and mostly everyone had real nice shines. Then I met a man with no color at all.

That's when we lived outside the little town of Misty, which hugs the line of Maximillian and the Southern Triangle, and still ain't decided which one it wants to be a part of. We farmed orchards with apples and oranges and fat bunches of grapes, and Mama had a vegetable garden that spat out vegetables bigger than anyone else's. She can make anything grow big and better tasting just with her hands.

We went to town with Mama sometimes, when she needed seeds or something else that couldn't wait for Daddy to get the next day. We'd walk down the dusty dirt roads, until we got close to the center of town where the roads turned into big flat stones cobbled together.

Every time we went to town, Mama stopped and bought us a lemonade at the corner store. It was so full of sugar it made a little coating on your teeth, that you could lick the rest of day, still taste the sweet. Mama ain't big on sweets, and it was always my favorite part. Carly always sipped hers all the way home, but I swallowed gulp after gulp until my throat seized up and sent needles through my head.

I was five the last time we ever went into Misty. It was real sunny that day, so bright I had to squint to see anything at all. We came on the man with a shiny black hat and matching coat right where the dust turned to stone. Under his hat, his face was pale and the way the sun was steaming off the pavement, it made his face blur, like it was melting right off. I squinted real hard, trying to see what kind of shade he was throwing off, but not a single color came off him.

"Mama," I said and tugged her hand. Me and Carly was on either side of her, our heads right at her waist even though Carly's four years older than me. Daddy says Mama and Carly are pint sized. Not like me and him.

"What?" Mama said, real irritated, pink with it. She got all nervous and twitchy when we came to town.

"That man ain't got no colors," I whispered.

His head turned real smooth and he smiled at me. Not at Mama and Carly, but at me. Underneath his glossy black mustache, his teeth were white and square and too big for his mouth. Looked fake. As we drew near, he bent at the waist like he was taking a bow, and said loud, "Hello, little girl! Would you like to see what I have inside my hat?"

"Yeah!" I said, tugged my hand free of Mama's, ran towards him.

"Grace!" Mama snapped and hustled after me.

The man took his hat off one handed and turned it upside down, passed his free hand over it in circles.

"Grace," Mama said, and I felt her fingers knifing into my shoulder. "Sir, we are late, no time for tricks, excuse us."

"We ain't late," I said. "I want to see."

The man dipped his hand in his hat and pulled out a fat white snake. It made an odd purring sound, and he looked at my Mama and smiled. I reached out and felt scales shiver soft and smooth.

"Come on, Grace," Mama said. She yanked on my shoulder.

The man closed his hand around the snake and dipped it back in his hat, Then he pulled it back out, and when he spread his fingers out there were three golden eggs, the same color as the little bubbles of light that came from Mama when she sang. "Little snakes are most often vulnerable in the egg, just like little birds in the nest," he told us.

"Grace!" Mama said, and this time she pulled harder, and I stumbled backwards, crying out 'cause it hurt. My mad mixed with my hurt feelings and floated away red and orange.

I went with her, my head turned around to look back at the colorless man. He was still smiling away. He kept his eyes on mine and leaned forward and blew a tiny snake from his mouth that landed on the middle egg. It hammered its triangle head into the shell and disappeared with its tail flicking back and forth.

"Turn around, Grace," Mama said, dragged me down the street. She held me so tight that I wore a purple wrist bracelet the next day.

"We never forget magic," the man called after us. "Not the kind that turned its back on its brothers!"

Mama's face got bone white and a real ugly color like wet ash circled her head. We didn't stop again, not for seeds, not even for lemonade.

"Why couldn't we see the magician?" I demanded. I was sparking yellow orange red.

We were on the dust roads leading out of town, and Mama stopped right in the middle of the road. She got down on her knees, looked at me and Carly real serious. Her color was a dark blue, twisted up with orange.

"That man wasn't a magician. He was a snake charmer," she said.

"What's a snake charmer?" Carly asked.

"It's a bad kind of magic," she said. "That's why we don't tell people about Grace seeing colors. Or about the light bubbles when I sing, or that I have the gift of growing. A long time ago, there was magic in a lot of places. But there was our kind of magic, the good kind, and then the dark magic. The snake charmers. Now, they didn't start as all bad. But sometimes they used their power to get things, when it wasn't fair to other people. And then people, the ones with no magic, became angry and scared. So, they chased the people with magic away, wouldn't sell things to them in town, wouldn't allow their children to go to school, that sort of thing. And then even people with good magic started hiding theirs, because they didn't want to get run off. Lots of the snake charmers died off. And the ones that were left, they had so much anger about being driven out, they turned mean as snakes. That's why people started calling them the snake charmers."

And she didn't say nothing else the way home. We got sent to our room so she could have peace and quiet. I heard her tell Daddy about the snake charmer as soon as he got home.

She was all kinds of colors, flashing red and blue and black and gold in pulses. "We can't stay here."

"Julia," Daddy said. "Maybe he was just a magician?"

"He had a snake come out his mouth, and crawl into the eggs the bird laid," I said. I was still supposed to be in my room.

"Grace," Mama said. "Room. Now."

I went to my room and closed the door loud, then tiptoed back out to listen.

"Maybe he's just passing through?" Daddy said. "He won't want people to catch onto him. I bet he's already moved on."

"You don't understand," Mama said. "Charmers hate my kind. He saw me, I know. He heard what Grace said. He'll come, and he won't stop coming until he's dead, maybe not even then, Nate. We have to go. Tonight. We have to run. I mean, I can grow anything. We'll go south where they don't mind a little magic as long as it don't hurt anyone. We make a new home."

There was a time when Daddy did anything Mama wanted. There was more talking but we left Misty that night.

It's funny but as time passed I sort of forgot the whole thing, even the awful bumpy midnight ride down here to South Song. It felt more and more like a dream if it did cross my mind.

First time I said anything about colors here, Mama shook her head. "Grace," she said. "It's time to stop being fanciful. There aren't any colors. It's just your imagination."

"No, it ain't," I said. "You made us move 'cause I didn't see no colors round that man, Mama." "That wasn't why," Mama said.

"But—"

"Grace," Mama said. "Stop arguing with me right now. I don't want to hear another word about colors, or I'll tan your little behind. There aren't any colors."

Bout that time was when Mama seemed to be finding wrong with anything I did. It felt like being slapped, knowing she knew I was telling the truth and she was saying it wasn't so.

I remember being so mad that my eyes stung with it. Ain't nothing worse than trying to say something and being told to shush.

I tried not seeing them. Not talking about them. But two days later I saw a woman with a big belly, when we went to town to get some things. I knew the lady was growing a baby inside her, but I don't get excited about that. What I got excited about was the bright pink web spinning out from her, clear into the sky. It was so damn pretty against the sky I couldn't breathe. "Mama!" I pointed above her head. "Look at the color!"

Mama's lips skinned tight against her teeth, turned pale white. She jerked my hand so hard I almost tripped. "Ssshh," she said, tinted a real ugly maroon.

When we got home, she made good on her hide tanning promise. I lay in bed the rest of the day with my eyes shut. Whenever I opened them, I saw ugliness.

You'd think I'd never have said a damn word about the colors ever again. I didn't talk about them, even to Carly. I tried to ignore them, and they started fading on me. It was tolerable enough, but sometimes I felt all hollowed out inside.

I was eight years old and two days when I seen Brian, a man my daddy's age, doing his limp down the street. He had gotten bucked off a horse a year before and it did something bad to his hip. He got sort of mean after that. He was always stained with a dark red hue if I looked real hard. His daughter Marley went to school with us, a real skinny girl with shiny blond hair. I didn't really know her 'cause she was almost sixteen. But people knew her daddy was bad on the drink, since the accident. People always got something to say about stuff like that.

This afternoon, I couldn't rightly see if he was on the drink, 'cause he was wrapped up in black so dark it looked wet. Like spilled ink all over his paper white skin. He was muttering to himself, too, looked crazy.

I felt ice cold looking at him all messy like that. I crossed the street so we didn't share the same side of the road. I went home and couldn't eat. I kept seeing that ink cloud. It had me wondering if things like that could leave the person they was on and come after other people.

Next day, Marley was just gone. Her mama went door to door, banging away, asking had anyone see Marley. My daddy went to town, to join the men who were going to search for her. I sat at the table and tried to tell Mama, about the ink cloud.

"Mama, I saw Marley's daddy in town yesterday," I said.

"And?"

"And he was walking down the street, and he scared me."

Mama stopped and looked at me. "What did he do?" she asked. "Was he on the drink again?"

"I don't know, ma'am," I said. "But he had real bad color around him like a cloud of real black—"

Mama took in some air, and when she blew it out, it was mad and scared, red and blue gray. "Goddammit, Grace," she whispered. Her eyebrows yanked down and a big fat line appeared in between them. "I have told you, and told you—"

"But Mama—"

"But nothing, Grace!" she roared. "Go to your damn room, right now!"

Mama tanned me again, worse. I stopped crying after the first couple licks, 'cause this mad feeling just sort of took over. *Ain't ever gonna let her see me cry again*, I promised myself. And when she was done, she was one crying. She knelt down beside me and she said, "Grace, this is for your own good. If you keep on talking about colors, people will get bad ideas. You have to forget about Brian, and Marley, and the colors. You hear me? You forget it all."

There's an old saying that there are some things better left forgotten, but that ain't right. There are things you should never forget. I knew I was seeing something important, but even that feeling sort of drifted away, faded like dreams do.

I don't like the new teacher. He smiles to greet us when we file into the big old school room that used to be a barn. It's the only building big enough to fit all of us, from the little kids still wiping snot on their sleeves, up to the older kids who only care about making big dumb moon eyes at each other. When he smiles, one of his lips curls up higher on one side, reveals big square teeth. It tugs at something in my head, but I don't know what. It's like everything faded with the colors.

The colors are little ghosts of their old selves, all faded and barely there. They only show up bright if it's real important. I guess looking at them sort of feels wrong, like peeping into other people's heads. There's some feelings people have that you don't want to see.

But Ellison ain't got no color, note even a hint of it, at all.

"I don't like him," I whisper to Carly.

Carly rolls her eyes. "Shut up and go sit down," she whispers back – "before you get us in trouble."

She shakes her hair as she walks down the side of the rows, like she's getting it behind her shoulders, but she's just doing it so everyone looks at her. She's real proud of all that golden hair she brushes one hundred times every morning and night. She likes being smart, but she likes being pretty more. She about pooped a kitten when she was voted the prettiest girl last year by the boys. They wrote her name on a piece of paper with little stars and hearts drawn around it, and she crowed about that all damn summer.

I didn't even make the pretty girl list, which Carly said was 'cause I was too young. She was being nice for once, but I don't care about that dumb list. You just know the girls who got excited about that are gonna pop out a hundred kids and get stuck right here in this dusty town where nothing ever happens. Me, I'm gonna be the first girl to ride to the North Border and back, just to show everyone I can. I'm gonna make history.

"I'm Mr. Ellison," the man says. Then he tells me, "Put that chair down on all four legs, Grace Milliken."

Then, he makes us change all our seats. We have to sit in the order of youngest to the oldest, which puts me in the front row. Stupid, 'cause I'm four inches taller than everyone in the second row. The front's for suck ups like Carly. I cross my arms and slouch when Ellison walks by, carrying a long, thin wooden pointer. He snaps it down on my leg right above the knee when he passes.

"Sit up straight, Grace Milliken," he says.

I ain't never been hit before by an adult, and I don't like it. It hurts, but worse, everyone saw it happen. I sit up straight and fold my arms across my chest, hot all through my face.

Everyone sits up arrow straight then. Nick's next to me looking out the side of his eyes and shrugging in sympathy. He ain't half bad, for a farmer boy. Ellison gets up to Carly's row, near the back since she's one of the oldest. Carly raises her hand. "Mr. Ellison, sir?"

Here we go. Everyone loves Carly 'cause she's just so *proper* and *perfect*.

"Yes, Carly?"

He already knows all our names on the first damn day. I don't like it, not at all.

"Sir, I can't see the board."

I sneak a look back, see James the 1st directly in front of her. There are two James, and this James is the big one, taller than anybody in class. Being short like she is, Carly can't probably see anything but the dirt on his neck. I snicker inside. Even if she can see, James the 1st's daddy has a hog farm and he's always stinking to high hell.

Mr. Ellison sighs. His noises are louder than his words. He's that kind of person.

I'm really lookinat him, how even the color around him looks faded. I want to tell someone, but I can't. Not anymore.

For being magic, Mama sure hates it. She can grow things just by touching them. When she sings, little bubbles of light float around her, but she pretends not to see them. My seeing colors ain't as good, 'cause I'm half ordinary like Daddy, but it's mine all the same. Carly can't do a lick of magic, but she's perfect in every other way. Everyone thinks so, except maybe Ellison, 'cause he just sighed at her.

That sigh Ellison makes, I see it hanging above Carly, see through but it's thicker than the rest of the air. I sit up a little, 'cause I ain't never seen that before.

"Are you saying I've made a poor choice, Carly, with my seating arrangements?" He smiles, his stupid lip curling up.

Carly flushes like I did. There ain't no right way to answer his question, and we all sort of wait to see what happens in the worst kind of quiet.

"No, sir, I was just- "

"Just what?" he slices into her mid-sentence. His eyes are squinted slits.

No one ever talks to Carly like that. She bites her lip, looking around, and I damn near feel sorry for her, but not sorry enough to stop thinking it was about time. *A little humility's good for the spirit,* Daddy said, the first time I fell off a horse and cried like a girl. *Makes you realize you ain't perfect.*

"No, sir," Carly whispers. She's staring at her hands in her lap. Her hair falls around her face. She's real pretty, like Mama. She's got little bones and big eyes, and big masses of long golden hair. Me, I'm tall and big through the shoulders like Daddy. Colored all different browns and tans, eyes and hair, average. I got robbed on that 'cause his good looks don't translate to my face.

"Are we going to have a problem this semester, Carly?"

He should let her alone after that, but he don't. He ain't smiling on the outside, but I think he is on the inside.

"No," she says, real soft.

"Stay when I dismiss the others," he says, and moves past her.

Carly's crying.

I feel bad, honest, but she's always been a crier.

I forget my lunchbox on purpose. I want to hear what that big galoot has to say to my sister. Just 'cause I don't always like her don't mean I stop looking out for her.

If she's got a fault, it's that she'll believe any damn thing people tell her. Three years she spent a whole week eating only potatoes when I told her they'd make her skin glitter. I heard it from this girl who had real pretty skin, said a boy up north wrote a song about it.

Or so she claimed. Me, I don't go around just believing any damn thing people say.

Carly's got her nose to the corner. I can see just the side of her face. Her cheek has old dusty tracks from the crying before. Ellison stands just a step away, no expression at all on his face. He's talking real intense, right in her ear. His words come out little colored snakes of yellow and green that slither into her ear. I strain my ears trying to catch what he says, but all I hear is hissing. The hissing is making me sick, like I might puke so hard breakfast comes out my nose. I feel hot and dizzy, so I get outside, where everyone's still sitting and eating. It can't have been long I was gone, but it felt like damn near forever.

Carly don't come out until I'm finishing my sandwich, trying to help my stomach stop turning flips.

She don't look no worse for the wear now, and don't stop to talk to me, so I mind my own business.

I don't say nothing about the snakes and Ellison to anyone. I'll just get tanned for it and no one will believe me anyway.

Carly nibbles at dinner and goes straight up to bed. When I get up to our room, she's standing there in her drawers, pinching at her stomach. She must have been doing it for a while, 'cause there are red blotches all along the top of her waist.

"What the hell you doing?" I ask.

"Don't curse, Grace," she says. She turns her head, looks at the back of her thigh. I see pinch marks there too. "I'm getting fat."

I snort. "You're real skinny. You're practically a walking skeleton. Why the hell would you think that, and why the hell you pinching yourself? Ain't nothing there but skin, and you're going stretch it all out doing that."

"You ought to start talking right," she says. "Otherwise people will think you're stupid. Anyway, it was just something someone said. Just forget it."

I go to bed thinking about how everyone always wants me to forget.

What do you think of the new teacher?" Dad asks at dinner next day.

"Hate him," I say.

"Grace!" Mama says. "Don't use that word."

"Well, what am I supposed to say? I do." I stab my fork into my potato, which splits down the middle. Me and Carly love potatoes. We both put a big fat pat of butter inside them and let it melt into the white stuff. "Pass me the butter, Carly."

"Strongly dislike," Mama says.

Carly pushes the butter plate over without taking any. She starts cutting her potato into tiny pieces. She puts one in her mouth and chews slowly.

"Not hungry?" Dad asks Carly.

"Well, someone at school told Carly she's fat, so she ain't eating," I say.

Mama frowns and Dad puts his fork down. "Who the hell called you fat?" Dad says.

"Well, where does Grace get it from, now?" Mama says to Dad, but it's just a reflex. She looks at Carly. "Carly, is that true?"

"No," Carly says. I see color in that lie, dirt brown, like shit. It's the first time in a couple years I seen a color that ain't all faded like old clothes and the first time I ever heard Carly lie.

"That's a goddamn lie!" I say real loud. I'm mad as hell. I can feel a whole bunch of things twisting around in my chest, wanting to come out.

"Grace!" Mama snaps, and this time I see her face beet red. I don't need to see nothing else to tell me she's mad. "You go to your room right now!"

"But she told a damn lie!"

"Get in your room Grace!" It comes out as dull red pulses. Seems like whenever Mama's got color, it's always at me, and it ain't never a nice color.

"This ain't fair, she doesn't even want to eat!" I holler, and stomp upstairs.

Dad comes up after a while. I paced around at first, but now I'm lying on my bed, still steaming. The bed dips when he sits down, rocks back and forth. He's a big, solid man. When he wraps his arms around Mama she practically disappears. "Hey kiddo," he says. "You know you can't curse like that."

"But she lied! You'd be pissed if someone lied on you too!" I glare at him.

"You sound just like your mama, you know. She was always getting all hot and bothered about something and getting herself in trouble."

"I don't believe you," I keep my face buried in the pillow. "Bet she was perfect, just like Carly's lying butt."

He laughs real low, says, "Aw, Grace, no one's perfect."

He pats me on the head and tells me to come finish dinner. I drag my feet on the stairs so everyone knows I'm still in my feelings about what happened. Mama's cleaning up and Carly's sitting at the table, most of her plate in front of her. I sit down and glare at her.

"Eat, Grace," Mama says without turning her head. Sometimes she knows what I'm doing without even looking. "And Carly, you're not done until you finish your plate."

I finish first, and get sent right back upstairs, which gets me mad all over again. Carly doesn't come up until it's dark, bedtime.

"You finally eat?" I snap at her, ready to fight.

"No," she says. She goes to bed without even brushing her hair. I lay there and look at my breath, steaming out maroon. It takes me a while to settle down, get to sleep.

I'm seeing colors again a lot. I don't like it.

Next day, Carly says she's sick and won't get out of bed. I go out with Mama and Dad and prune trees in the orchard, and then we all come in and play a game of cards. If I could see my colors now, I know they'd be all sky blue right now. I like it being the three of us sometimes.

"You giving up on your good looks?" I ask Carly, walking to school. She only brushed her hair a couple times this morning and didn't pinch her cheeks or run her finger through the jam and paste it to her lips either. "You ain't hardly brushed your hair."

"Why should I?" Carly says. She's walking with her head tilted to the side, like I do when I get water in my ear. "No one cares what my hair looks like when I'm this fat."

She's skinny as ever. "You ain't fat," I tell her.

"They say I am," she says, still walking with her head craned almost to her shoulder.

"Who? What the hell is the matter with you?" I like the way that sounds coming out. Dad says that to Mama when she gives him a hard time about his ales at night. A sharp-edged joke.

"Do you hear that?" Carly says instead of answering.

"Hear what?"

"The birds," she says. She stops and turns in a circle real slow. "Their wings. The talking."

"What birds?" The road we walk to school on is bare of trees, just a dusty stretch of road leading to a dead end.

"They're everywhere," she whispers. "In here." She taps her head. I see color starting to appear around her. She's the color of fireplace ashes and embers.

I don't know what to do or say. After a minute she just walks on.

I trail behind her, inspecting the sky for anything with wings.

Day 4, Carly don't spell wicked right, leaves the c out. Ellison keeps her in for recess. I sneak in but he isn't hissing this time. Instead, Carly sits at her desk, every part of her bowed over. He sits at his desk, with his fingers steepled together. His smile a mean curve to his face, and all the color in the room is gone. Not just from him but gone from the walls and books and plants.

"Something's wrong at school," I tell Dad. He's started in on the dead orchard trees lying in pieces behind the orchard. He strips them of their bark, sands them down, makes things. He don't never know what he's gonna do until it takes its own shape. He says things want to be made.

"Bad wrong?" he asks.

Dad asks one question, and listens. Mama asks a hundred and don't.

"Yeah," I say. "It's Ellison. He hates Carly. He keeps her inside for lunch all the time and I think he says mean things to her."

"Mean things like what?" Dad stops and rests his hands on the tree between his legs.

"I don't rightly know the exact words," I tell him. "I just know he does."

"She tells you that?"

"I went back inside for my lunch first day," I say. "He was in her ear, talking real quiet."

"He yell? Or put his hands on her?"

"No, sir," I say.

"But it made you scared? Or scared for Carly?"

"Made me mad, but made me fearful, sir."

"Gracie," he says. He put his hands on his hips. "Did he tell Carly she was fat?"

"I don't rightly know," I say. I hesitate, try to think how to explain it the thing I can't explain. "He's not a good person, Daddy. I can tell, you know I can. I think he's bad. Real bad."

"Gracie," he put his hand on my shoulder. "I believe you. You know why?"

"Why?"

"You ain't said a damn swear word this whole time," he says. He smiles, but he has to work at it. "I'll take care of it, kiddo. Alright?"

"Yes, sir," I nod. I get a bad feeling, but I don't know why. It's sort of like I know I got a big boulder rolling, but I don't know where it's going. I don't feel like talking anymore, and I turn to leave.

"Gracie?" Dad says. "You see any colors round him?"

We don't talk about the colors since Mama said not to.

"If I see them, they're not good ones," I say, but I don't wait to see his reaction. He wants to talk about colors if it was about Carly. That sort of sticks somewhere in me, but I ain't going to tell anyone about it.

"What the hell did you say?" Carly comes at me, and I'm faster than her but the cursing froze me. Violet clouds erupt from her nostrils and scatter. It scares me, what I'm seeing.

"Hell!" I throw up my arms to protect my face, but she don't swing, pushes me down on my bed instead. My head hits the wall, and I push back at her. "What the *goddamn hell*, Carly?"

"You tell Dad or Mama?" she snaps.

"Tell 'em what?"

"About me getting in trouble at school." Her eyes are jumping out of her head, crazy like her hair's getting.

"I didn't say nothing about you getting in trouble," I say. "I said that damn Ellison is mean to you."

"That's getting in trouble!" Carly says. Big fat tears start slipping out of her eyes. "I ain't nothing but trouble!"

"That's a goddamn stupid thing to say," I tell her. "Ellison say that?"

She glares at me. "He doesn't say a goddamn thing to me, understand?"

"Liar," I whisper.

She pushes me again, and this time my head cracks the wall good. All my air gusts out and I ain't even mad. She's lost her damn mind. I want to get good and mad, but I'm sort of scared to. I ain't never seen someone shoot sparks from inside like she is.

"You just mind you own business," she said, up so close her words lash my face. "You little spoiled *bitch*."

I don't say nothing after that. Don't change into my bedclothes either. I just crawl under my sheets, pull them to my neck, and stare at the ceiling wishing I could make pretty colors that flowed and painted over the bad ones. It's a long time before I close my eyes.

Carly don't say a word to me walking to school. She walks the whole time with her head tilted, frowning. A kaleidoscope of darkness spinning webs from her. I wish the colors would go away.

Daddy comes walking into school just before lunch. Ellison sees him but don't stop talking about the old Gods. Yesterday he said how the old Gods abandoned their people, left them with special powers that the people from before didn't like. How the people decided they would get rid of people who were different, how they drove them off and murdered them and stole their children. Beat anything different right out of them. But he said there was something called full circle which meant that what goes around comes around. He drew on the chalkboard a snake in a circle eating its own tails.

But today he talks about the same stuff our other teachers did. About history, how often people used to worship their Gods, how some of them still have old paintings and books they read out of every day, blah blah blah.

Daddy leans up against the wall against the back of the classroom, his arms folded across his chest, listening. I sneak a look back at Carly, who's either so mad she erased it off her face, or scared. I can't tell but I feel smooth as a turquoise sea, 'cause my Daddy's a man takes care of things.

Ellison dismisses us and walks right up to Daddy, extends his hand. They shake hands, but Daddy takes a minute to do it. He holds that slimy hand, half the size of his, and they look each other up and down.

"Mr. Milliken, I presume?" Ellison nods at me, waiting. "Your daughter is a fierce likeness."

"In more ways than one," Daddy says. He let go of Ellison, looks at me. "Go on outside, Gracie. You too, Carly."

Ellison's lips skim his teeth, peel back. Both sides, but I look real close at his mouth and see the side that usually curls up twitching away under his skin.

I hate waiting. When Daddy strides out, he don't seem no different. He says goodbye to Carly, kisses her on top of the head, then pulls me alongside him. He keeps his voice real low when he speaks.

"That man," he says, just to me. "or any other, for that matter, is not to keep you or Carly at lunch or after school, ever, by yourselves. You hear me? He tries to, you come right home and get me. You understand Gracie?"

"Yes, sir," I say.

"Now go on," he says. "I'll be here to walk you girls home."

I go in feeling smug, like I won, and then I see little tendrils of smoke coming off Ellison. He's thick with them, and I feel more scared than mad just like that. All his face is tight, like it's being sucked in, cheekbones knives ready to slice through the flesh and let the real him out.

He's a man with no color. He's a snake charmer. I guess I knew it, sort of. You know how you know something, but you ain't ready to believe it? Like maybe your Mama likes your sister better, but you just pretend she don't? It's the kind of knowing you pretend ain't there.

Me and Carly get sent right to our room so Mama and Dad can talk. Carly don't want to listen, but I do. I press my ear against the door and I hear them talking real urgent. I wished I could see what their words are wearing, but I'm cutoff from what's happening, and I hate it. I got to tell them about the rest of it, how Ellison's got the black magic. I want to know exactly what is going to happen, so I can rein in this damn fear horse thundering through me.

The sun dips low before they call us down. Mama's pinned her pale hair back and her eyes have gone from bright blue to dark. She's fidgeting like I do at school. Daddy's sitting sideways in his chair, elbow resting on the table.

"I know you two must want to know what's going to happen," Mama says.

"This is so stupid," Carly says, crying. She's got more of a water supply than anybody I know. "Nothing happened."

"Hell, it didn't," Daddy says. His eyes are narrow in his face. He's looking at

Carly like he maybe wants to smack her, which I feel in my bones. "I don't know what's been going on down at that school, but you aren't acting right, Carly."

"Ellison, he's a snake charmer," I say. I'm so scared I'm shaking, but I gotta get this out. "I know it. He's like that man we ran away from. He hissed snakes right in her ear!"

"You don't know a damn thing," Carly says. "You think you're so smart, everyone does, but you're *not*."

"We're not arguing," Mama says. "We're not even discussing. Until we get this handled, neither of you are going to school."

"But that's not fair!" Carly bursts out, hollering. "IT'S NOT FAIR!" and she just screams it over and over until it blurs into one long continuous color flashing desperation at us. Then her limbs go boneless and she flops onto the floor, crying. Mama gets down to her knees beside her.

"But it's the only time the birds are quiet," Carly moans.

"What birds?"

"The ones in my head," Carly says. "All day and all night, they beat their wings inside me and I can hear it in words in my head, they're saying the most terrible things, and it only stops there, at school."

Dad and Mama look at each other, over Carly unspooled on the floor. I think they might tell me to go to my room, but I think they forgot me. There's only the three of them—the broken one, and the scared adults.

"What do they say?" Mama asks, real nice. Her voice molasses over pancakes, so sugar sweet it makes my teeth ache. "Carly, darling, tell me what the birds say."

"Fat," Carly whispers. "Ugly. Stupid. Worthless. Good for nothing. They tell me I'll have to be a whore because I can't do anything at all, and I'll be bad at it, because I'm so fat and ugly."

There's a great crack through the room and we all jump. Even Dad himself, who looks at the big seam that now runs down the table. His fingers are white knuckles of rage.

Mama gets Carly calmed down, carries her to their bed. Dad paces. She comes out and she tells me to sleep in their bed with Carly. I tell her no, don't leave me with Carly. I'm whining, near tears.

"You take care of your sister, now, Grace," she says. She kisses me on the top of the head. She looks at me. "I'm awful proud of you, Grace. You're very brave. Like your father."

I go in and lay next to silent Carly, on top of the sheets. Her body curves away from me, a slivered half-moon against the sheets. I lay board stiff next to her, thinking about the whores. I guess I never did think about them before. I know about sex, and stuff. I mean, I'm eleven and I have an older sister who's kissed boys but nothing else. I ain't even sure what a whore is, except it's a woman who does sex type stuff with lots of men.

I know that's how we came from Mama and Dad too. Mama told us the first time Carly asked. *We made you with our bodies*, she said, and thinking about now, in their bed makes me feel hot and uncomfortable. They ain't always quiet about it, but it's always when I'm supposed to be sleeping, so I can't rightly complain. But I feel odd, thinking about it now.

I get up and sit at the edge of the bed. I can hear Mama and Daddy talking about moving away again. Carly has her eyes closed, maybe sleeping. I reach over and brush her hair like Mama did to calm her down. She doesn't stir but then my fingers brush up against something hard.

I tug it out a knot, but it's not hair.

It's a feather.

Carly pitches a fit this morning. I wake up when her feet drum the bed and little rat a tat tats run down her spine, which curves unnatural. I scream until Dad and Mama come. Dad freezes statue still, but Mama comes and gathers Carly in her arms. She starts to sing, first just a melody from words I know. Then the song glows and spins. The words stretch and change until I can't recognize them, getting long and dancing around the room, rainbows spinning in little circles.

Carly's body stops shaking and she's limp in Mama's arms.

Dad's moving again, a big tree of a man trembling like a leaf. "Julia," he says. "We should just pack up and go. Right now."

"It's too late," Mama says. "He's already got inside her somehow."

Daddy's twisting his hands together and they're turning red. "What, then?"

Mama looks at him. "It won't stop, Nate."

"Alright," Daddy says. "Alright."

The space between them uncurls and fills with black ink.

Daddy leaves then.

Mama and I clean up Carly, starting with her hair. Mama gives me her comb and she takes Dad's and we tease the ends out first. It takes some doing, but with slow small strokes, we get most of the tangles out without cutting it.

"Mama?" I say.

"Gracie?" she makes it a question.

"He did it. Ellison put the birds in her head. The first day. I went back to get my lunch and he was saying something to her, and I could see his words like snakes go right in her ear. I should have told you, huh? You could have fixed it?"

"Oh, Grace," she says. She stops and hugs me right against her.

I'm as tall as her, and wider still, but she still circles me up somehow.

"I wouldn't have listened, probably," she says. "You know? Sometimes I don't listen."

"I know," I say, and she squeezes tighter.

"You haven't hugged me in so long," she murmurs.

"Where's Daddy?" I ask.

Her body goes stiff. She lets go and I don't need colors to tell me she's ashamed and scared and defiant all at the same time. I guess 'cause I feel all them feelings too. I knew it when she told Daddy to go. I seen blackness stretched between them, the kind where there ain't no light at all.

"He went to kill Ellison," I say. I know it's true. I feel a real blackness inside me too, thick and ugly, squeezed up round my heart.

"The connection has to be broken," Mama says. "By any means necessary. You saw Carly this morning. She could die."

"I ain't saying its wrong," I say. "What's Daddy mean? It never ends?"

"You can't make it go away, any kind of magic. It just takes another shape."

"Why though?" I ask. "Why us?"

Right then, Carly sits up. She has half her hair smooth as melted butter and half a huckleberry bush. Her eyes are wide and there ain't nothing in them. She opens her mouth and I think she's gonna scream but birds start spilling out of her mouth. Blackbirds, owls, little gray and red plumed birds, too big for her. They come and come and Mama screams. I don't think but I jump up and run to the big window. I shove it open, catching splinters in all my fingers. The birds beat their wings without stopping, going right through a window way too damn small for their size and number, but it happens.

Outside they caw and beat and their wings make a hard rain sound. It softens as they begin to move farther off.

Carly collapses back on the bed and lies still.

I miss my Daddy so fierce I could die right now.

Mama puts her head down and sobs.

I go to the floor and put my head down and don't.

We all pretend things are fine, now.

Dad came home vacant eyed to Carly sitting up, talking. She didn't remember a damn thing. Mama was petting her, the way you do a fresh kitten. I was squeezing my hands together, blind to the fact blood was dripping from all them splinters. Daddy was washing blood off his hands when I felt mine aching, saw the mess I'd made. I sort of gasped, and Daddy saw the splinters. He sat me down and took each splinter out like I might break, and when he was done, he laid his head against the table and sobbed.

We all broke in some way, I guess.

Dad doesn't come home until late now. Sometimes, he smells like other women. Mama and he argue about it, and sometimes they make noise after but it isn't quiet and it isn't nice. Once I very clearly heard Mama say 'hurt me, then'. I want to tell you he didn't.

Carly acts like nothing happened. I asked her once what she remembered and she told me to leave her alone. I tried to see what colors lurked inside her but after I saw murder coloring my mama and daddy, I never saw them again. Carly's been seeing this boy from the next town over who has a whole bunch of money. She says she's getting out of this place.

I guess I'm different now too. I don't feel like the same person. I don't curse or see colors. I try to find them in people and places, but everything's gone flat and dull.

I hear hissing in my sleep, and I'm afraid it's not a dream. I dream about birds, lined up on house roofs, beady black eyes and sharp beaks. I dream of snake pits, dozens of snakes slithering over each other in knots and wake up with my heart running double time.

I found a black crow feather under my window pillow this morning.

If I'm really quiet, I hear wings fluttering all around.

I'm afraid. And I miss all the colors I cannot see.

See L'Erin Ogle's story "All the Colors I Cannot See" online at Metaphorosis.
If you liked it, leave a comment. Authors love that!
Remember to subscribe to our e-mail updates so you'll know when new stories are posted.

About the story

"All the Colors I Cannot See" began with the idea I had that a man hissed snakes into a girl's ear. The snakes laid eggs, hatched into birds, and drove the girl mad. Grace then became the central character as the story came out, because I wanted to have the narrator as an observer of the character being driven mad.

I was surprised by the ending myself, how dark the piece got. It surprised me by how pervasive the evil was, how it was fluid, getting in through every crack.

This was one of my favorite stories to write and Grace one of my favorite characters.

A question for the author

Q: Are you an outline or discovery writer?

A: Discovery! I usually start with an idea and then it takes on a life on my own. The story usually tells itself. Some stories barely resemble my original idea.

About the author

L'Erin is a writer from Lawrence, Kansas. She writes when she's not saving lives at her other job. She can be found online at lerinogle.com

@lerinjo

Not All Those Who Wander Are Lost

Douglas Anstruther

-1-

Carla sat on the edge of the metal railing that lined the motel's third-floor landing, gripping its paint-chipped bars with long, slender legs. Black lace stockings disappeared into a tattered bathrobe and a lipstick-stained cigarette rested between her fingers.

She liked the feel of the breeze on her legs, the thrill of the twenty-foot drop below. She wasn't a danger junkie, far from it, although she could have probably found a safer way to make some cash while Ash was at school — a florist, maybe, or a cashier. She had job offers, but the hours weren't flexible enough, and cashiers got robbed all the time anyway.

"So." The man standing behind her cleared his throat. "Are you married?"

"Me? Nah. Never tried it." She looked back at him. "How about you?" She thought he'd said his name was Stig, but she wasn't about to use it. Guys didn't like it when you got their name wrong, even if it was fake.

He stared past her into the mid-day heat rising from the oil-stained and cracked parking lot. He was kinda cute, like a movie star from the nineteen fifties: chiseled jaw, dimpled chin and blond curly hair. His stained and wrinkled dress pants contrasted with the smooth skin of his chest. A patch covered his left eye.

"Yeah," he answered in a faraway voice. "I think so."

"You think so?" A column of ash fell from her cigarette to splash across the cars parked below. "You mean you don't know?"

"I lost her. I lost them all. Two sons and a wife. I'm trying to find them, though."

She looked at him, her face a squint as she took a drag of her cigarette. "Whadya mean?" Her words came out with a cloud of smoke. "You *misplaced* them?"

"The places I go." He paused, shaking his head. "It gets complicated."

A new sadness in his eye caused her attitude to soften. She liked the guy. He seemed nice, and there was something mysterious about him. He came across somewhere between a world-weary sailor and a lost child: just a first impression, but she was usually right. "Look, I'm sorry. I, uh, I hope you find them." She stubbed out the cigarette and shrugged the bathrobe down a few inches, revealing breasts swept by the ends of her long black hair. "So, you ready to go again?"

After, she fell off him, scooped her bathrobe up from the floor, and headed to the TV in search of the remote, threading her hands into oversized armholes on the way. She always brought her own bathrobe. It was portable luxury: armor against the squalor of the cheap motels that even the sticky remote couldn't pierce.

She returned to the bed, settled back against the headboard and started pushing buttons. The TV remained black, and after a few seconds she sighed and tossed the worthless device onto the bedstand with a clatter.

At the sound, the man sat upright like a sprung trap. He frowned at the remote, then sank down and stared at the ceiling. As he moved, Carla briefly saw the black silhouette of a raven tattooed at the base of his neck. The image recharged his air of mystery and piqued her curiosity. She remembered their discussion on the landing; maybe exploring some of his secrets would be even more interesting than her missed shows.

"So, where did you see them last?" she asked.

"Hmm?"

"Your family. Where was the last place you saw them?"

"It's not really like that. It's that I can't find the path back to them."

"What do you mean, 'the path back to them'? Were you camping or something?"

He looked at her, measuring her up in a way she'd seen before. She recognized the instant he decided that she wasn't important enough to lie to. She didn't like the look. It took something from her, and the secrets the johns told her, usually how they hated their kids or planned to leave their wives, weren't worth the cost.

"I travel through time," he said. "That's where I lost them: among the possible timelines."

"What?" Her sardonic expression went unnoticed, unable to penetrate his study of the ceiling.

"I move forward in time, look around, go back, change something and then when I move forward again things are different. The possibilities form an immense branching tree, and I lost them somewhere in its branches."

"Seriously? You've been to the future?" She leaned in and conjured a seductive voice harvested from a lifetime of movies. "Do you know what happens to me?"

"A little."

"Prove it." She flounced against him on the bed, now playing little girl. "Tell me something about my future."

"You're going to steal my wallet when I take a shower in five minutes."

"Pfft, that's some reverse psychology bullshit. I'm not gonna touch your wallet."

He just stared ahead and shrugged.

"C'mon," she said, disappointed he wasn't playing. "Tell me something better. You know, like a fortune teller."

"Your son, Ash. He's going to die in three weeks."

All her voices and personas fell away like chips from a poker table thrown over before a bar fight. She peeled herself from him while wide-eyed shock slid into an angry glare. "That's not funny," she said with a dire tone. He kept staring at the ceiling, oblivious or unconcerned. "Hey. I said that's not funny!" She shoved him, but he gave no response. His calm indifference was a stiff breeze against her kindled anger but she didn't know what to do. Finally, after crouching in a frustrated rage for several seconds, she threw herself off the bed, snatched her cigarettes from the bedstand and stormed outside, slamming the door behind her.

A few minutes later, she returned to find the bed empty and the sound of running water coming from the bathroom door. She changed quickly into her clothes, stuffed the bathrobe into her massive purse and headed out. Before the door closed she paused, went back inside and wrestled the wallet from the man's jeans, where they lay in a heap by the side of the bed. She slammed the door again as she left.

It wasn't until that night that she realized he had used her son's name.

-2-

The roar of machinery forced their tiny guide to conduct the entire tour by shouting. The young woman, transformed into a bright orange blob by layers of safety gear, led her three charges through a maze of complex and expensive-looking equipment.

The company's Chief Technical Officer, a tall woman in her mid-thirties, had joined Stig and Osmond to answer questions that never materialized. Osmond couldn't remember the CTO's name. He figured her real role was to tackle him or Stig if either started taking pictures of their proprietary do-hickeys. She had somehow managed to retain a feminine shape despite the safety gear, and Osmond considered testing his theory, but he knew that Stig would make a scene soon enough and he didn't want to interfere.

Dr. Stig Gangleri, his best friend since college, and co-owner of Aesir Consulting, managed to look good in the gear too. It contributed to a mystic shaman vibe, with his bright blue eyes shining through the protective glasses like twin beacons of magical enlightenment. Osmond's own gear had consigned him to Club Blob, along with their guide.

They followed the guide through a vast underground warehouse filled from floor to ceiling with twisting, brightly colored pipes and tanks. Osmond only heard half of what the guide said and understood even less, but it didn't matter. Stig was the show pony. Osmond only made it happen, then made sure Stig didn't get lost on the way home.

"Temperature and pressure are all monitored remotely, as you can see here." The tour guide looked back at the group and paused. "Dr. Gangleri?" She looked around, causing Osmond and the CTO to do the same. Stig had disappeared.

They scattered to look for their missing companion and eventually found him in an aisle they had passed earlier, with his arms crossed and head tilted back, staring blankly at the bend of a pipe.

"He hasn't listened to a word I've said," the guide said, exasperated.

"What's he looking at?" the CTO asked.

"Oh, probably nothing," Osmond offered. "He gets like that sometimes. His mind takes him somewhere else entirely, but trust me, this is your man."

No one seemed particularly interested in going to get him, expecting instead that their collective stare would bring him back in line. Osmond knew different, but was in no hurry. He didn't want to ruin the magic.

"What are his credentials again?" the guide asked, incredulous.

"The professor has PhDs in both theoretical physics and statistical analysis."

"Hmph," the guide said, still unhappy that her shouting had been in vain.

"But it's not the credentials that matter. My associate has a photographic memory and an amazing gift for extrapolation and leaps of intuition. He's a genius the likes of whom you've never seen."

"He doesn't look like he could put his shoes on in the morning," the guide muttered.

"Hey now, show some respect!" All eyes turned to Osmond, who found himself glowering over the petite guide like a great ape defending his territory.

"Sorry. Sorry. It's just that—" He shook his head and tore away from their stares to look back at Stig. "He's a great man. You'll see."

They shuffled in place awkwardly for several minutes before Stig broke free and wandered back to the group, unaware or unconcerned that they had been waiting.

The tour guide resumed with a sigh. "Dr. Gangleri, thank you so much for joining us." Her eyes flashed to Osmond, whose affable smile deflected her sarcasm. "What I had been *trying* to explain is that data from the remote sensors is actually processed at the—"

"At the point of collection, the same way the retina and many other biological sensors process data." Stig finished her sentence to hijack the conversation, then promptly changed the subject. "You will have a seam failure in three days. It will begin there." He pointed at a structure in an aisle they hadn't reached yet. "It will cause one death and nine million dollars in damages."

"With all due respect, Dr. Gangleri," the guide said in a tone suggesting any debt of respect had been fully settled, "if you had paid attention, you would know that a failure of that nature is impossible because—"

"Because all seams are robotically resistance-welded within a tolerance of point zero one percent. That doesn't matter. Material strain from micro-temperature fluctuations will lead to the failure." With arms still folded across his chest he walked briskly down another aisle toward a section they hadn't visited. After a few seconds, the rest of the group caught up. The guide's face glowed red beneath the plastic shield and the CTO had a look of intrigued skepticism. Osmond tried and failed to suppress a grin. He always enjoyed seeing Stig do his thing.

Suddenly, Stig stopped and pointed at what seemed a random direction. "That pile has a heat leak which is throwing off your calibration. It won't be caught for three months and will result in the loss of a major grant."

Then he swung around and pointed to a drain grate on the floor. "Rats. A sink overflow upstairs at the end of the year will lead to an infestation. It'll never be discovered, but the ammonia from their urine will slowly degrade the sensors and prevent you from ever achieving the project goal."

The guide and the CTO both stood stunned, mouths agape. Osmond smiled broadly. "And there you have it," he said. "You will, of course, find Dr. Gangleri's predictions to be one hundred percent accurate. Payment has already been confirmed and no refunds are available. However, I assure you, none will be needed."

The CTO straightened herself and turned to Osmond, "I look forward to Dr. Gangleri's report, especially the technical analysis that supports his conclusions."

"Oh, my dear." Osmond wrapped his orange arm around her shoulders. "There will be no report. Our work here is done. You've been pointed in the right direction; the rest is up to you. One word of advice, though: if you can't figure out how he's right, assume he is anyway, okay? Best avoid that death and all that wasted money." He dropped his grin and looked at her steely-eyed. His voice took on a serious edge. "He's *never* wrong."

He released the stunned CTO and moved over to Stig, placing his gloved hand on his friend's back to direct him toward the exit. "Thank you, we really must be going now."

"But, Dr. Gangleri," the CTO called out as the two men moved away. "How do you know all this?"

Stig stopped and turned. "I saw it happen."

-3-

Stig walked down the short hall that divided living room from kitchen. It was always the same house with the same familiar smell of old wood and the same creaking floors, even if *he* wasn't always the same. The thought sent his hand rising up unconsciously toward his healthy left eye.

He had grown up here and inherited the place from his grandmother on his twenty-first birthday. He had been happy in this house: in the past, as a child doted on by his grandmother who had raised him as her own, and again, in a future he couldn't find. The rest of the time, its emptiness felt like a cold that the heaters couldn't warm.

Sometimes, when he turned the corner into the living room he didn't know if he would find his grandmother sunk into her old overstuffed chair reading spy novels or his sons sprawled across the floor playing while his wife watched sleepily from the couch.

This time, the room was empty except for hundreds of sheets of paper that covered the floor. His heart sank. He had no reason to expect otherwise, but hope grew from a different place than reason.

He walked into the room, stepping carefully on the edges of the pages, which puckered between foot and carpet as he went. Each page contained a portion of an immense branching map of the possibilities he had explored. He remembered them all perfectly, every detail of every moment. Yet nowhere in this map could he find his family. His memories of them were as vivid as any of the branches beneath his feet, but somehow they had become detached from the tree of possibilities. He couldn't find his way back to them. He had lost them.

He knelt down among the pages and traced each branch, looking for a lead, a promising direction to explore. He had recited this mantra a thousand times before. It had become an invocation, a prayer to be happy again.

A loud knock at the door interrupted his reverie. There he found Osmond Higgins, always best friend and sometimes business partner, fidgeting on the step. Osmond was a big man with a ruddy, pock-marked face and gaps between his teeth. He gave Stig a wide smile and a bone shaking pat on the back.

"Hey, Stig. I need some papers signed and wanted to drop off this check." He marched past Stig toward the kitchen. "That last gig was great. They already confirmed two of your predictions, and I gotta say they are loving you now. Word of mouth, my friend, word of mouth. That's what will send us into the heavenly realm of outrageous consulting fees." He opened the refrigerator and closed it with a grunt of disappointment. "Do you even eat?" He turned to Stig and smiled, "How are you doing, buddy?"

"Good," Stig answered, wandering back to the living room.

"How's your, uh, project going? What did you call this again?" Osmond asked, following his friend into the paper-strewn room.

"It's Yggdrasil. The tree of life."

"Right. All the possible futures you've explored, looking for your, uh, family. It's a lot bigger than the last time I was here. You've been busy."

Osmond stood back and squinted at the mighty opus. Through sheer artistic accident, the heavily annotated branching connections did look like a massive gnarled tree, spread across several hundred pieces of paper. Cramped, looping symbols inscribed along its length lent it a texture of mossy bark and hundreds of tiny oval notes dangled from the branches like leaves. The entire left side was stunted and dark, as if the great tree had been hit by lighting. There, the symbols crashed into each other with a sense of urgency, giving the branches a scarred, sinister appearance.

"What are the leaves, again?"

"Decision points. Variables that are likely to significantly alter subsequent events."

"Um, in English?"

Stig sighed. "Possible directions of future exploration."

"I see. And where are we now? What branch or twig or whatever shows us having this conversation?"

Stig pointed to a spot near the upper right edge of the tree. "We're here."

Osmond nodded and leaned forward. "May I?"

Stig motioned for him to proceed. "Carefully."

"Of course."

Osmond tip-toed between the pages, careful not to disturb any. The page Stig pointed to looked like all the others. Thick dark lines connected it to the surrounding pages. Strange symbols and occasional words, places and names crowded around the lines. Stig had once tried to explain his personal system of time-travel notation, but Osmond had retained nothing.

Osmond looked up. "Well, I don't understand it, but it looks pretty impressive."

"It's a rough map. A way for me to see how the pieces fit together as I explore the timelines, following leads, looking for them."

He looked down at the great tree on the floor, superimposing it over the one in his mind. He could move through it much the same as in the trees he had climbed as a child. With almost no effort, he could release his grasp of the present and slide down to another time, catch himself on the crook of a past fork, then pull himself onto a different branch using memories as footholds, until he reached its terminus, where time would resume its measured growth. He had clambered over every inch of the tree but couldn't find his family. His recollections of them, although intense, were as unsubstantial as sunlit mists, and wouldn't support his weight.

"What are all those branches that start behind us? Like those over there." Osmond pointed to the left side of the tree.

"Those branches are what happens when I drop out of college."

Osmond shivered like a teenager at a campfire ghost story. "You mean 'if you had' dropped out of college. I was at your graduation, all of them. So, those other branches never happened. You know that, right?"

Stig shrugged. "I still go there. Those branches are as real as any other."

"My friend," Osmond said, "don't you see? You aren't time traveling. You're daydreaming. I once read that Henry Ford could design a machine and then run it in his mind. You're like that, except the machine you're running is the world. You imagine alternate pasts and possible futures with such detail that you feel like you're there, living them, but the entire time you're really here, in the present, with the rest of us, running simulations.'

"Maybe," he said, with a patience that bordered on boredom.

Osmond shook his head and scanned the left half of the tree. "Honestly, I'm not sure it's healthy for you to keep going back there. It's like you're building entire fantasy worlds and then living in them."

Osmond had expressed these concerns in every timeline. To him, only the timeline he was on was real and all others were the products of Stig's overactive imagination. Stig understood that — his friend couldn't travel from one to another, he couldn't see that no present had more claim on reality than any other. The surety of experience inoculated Stig from doubt, but each time Osmond raised the question, he received another dose of the contagion and there were times when he wondered if maybe Osmond were right. Perhaps he had lost more than his family. Perhaps he had lost the present.

"Hey, I see the name Carla a lot over here. Is that the woman you've been looking for? Your wife?"

"No. Just an acquaintance."

"Well, you'll have to introduce me to her someday. You know, if she's real."

-4-

"Excuse me. Sir? Mr. Gangleri!" The voice came from his blind spot but didn't startle him. Stig finished threading the key into the front door of his house then turned toward the road. A woman hurried toward him from the other side of the street. She looked like a stressed-out soccer mom, with frazzled, pulled-back hair, and jeans tucked into boots that made for awkward running. He traced her path back to an old Honda Civic where cigarette butts on the ground attested to a long wait.

"I'm not sure if you remember me." she said, breathless from her short jog. "I'm—"

"Carla Munn. From the motel." He turned back to the door lock. "I remember."

"You, uh, left this. At the motel." She produced a bulging flap of leather and held it out to him straight-armed. "It's all still there."

Stig took the wallet, tucked it into his back pocket and walked inside, leaving the door open behind him. Carla glanced back at her car for a moment before following him into the dark house and closing the door behind her. She found Stig in the kitchen, filling a glass of water.

He leaned against the counter, glass in hand, and watched her. He could see her unease, her keen awareness that she was in the middle of someone else's house, no longer on neutral ground. For all of her daring and bravado, she wouldn't be here without a good reason.

"Look, I don't," she stopped and shook her head. "This sounds crazy, but I need your help. It's my boy, Ash." Her eyes started to fill and her voice cracked. "He's dying." She burst into tears and sat heavily at the kitchen table, sobbing. Stig leaned against the sink taking occasional sips from his glass. He wanted to console her, but it would be awkward, strange. He didn't need to visit the future to see that.

"You knew it was going to happen," she said, her voice an octave higher than usual. "Somehow you knew."

Slowly her sobbing subsided and with a determined face, streaked with mascara and snot, she collected herself and continued. "Two weeks ago, Ash spent the afternoon playing with his cousin." She paused for a moment to search her purse for a tissue which she unfolded and used to wipe her face. "Three days later Ash got a real bad headache, a high fever and a weird rash. Later we found out his cousin had been sick too but got better on his own. Ash just kept getting worse. I've never seen anyone so sick. At the hospital they put him on a breathing machine. They said he had meningitis." She started to tear up again. "Now they say my little boy is brain dead and they want to pull the plug. Mister Gangleri, you've got to help him."

Stig set the empty glass on the counter and frowned. Her formality always caught him off guard, but what did he expect? She didn't know all the times they'd been together, all the permutations. Carla was a recurring feature of these timelines, the forbidden fruit of the dark side of the tree. To her, he would be little more than a stranger, a one-time customer, but he knew her well and thought of her, in a strange way, as a friend.

She stood up and grabbed his sleeve. "Did you hear me? You've gotta do something. You said you time travel or something. You could prevent this. Please."

Stig spoke dryly. "If I were to go back and prevent his death, it would create a new timeline. This branch would still exist. He'll still die here."

"Take me with you, then."

He shook his head. "I'm sorry, Carla. But it doesn't work that way."

"I don't care!" she shouted. "At least in some other universe or whatever, my baby will live. I don't care. Please, save him. I'll do anything, *anything*." She moved her hand up and ran her fingers jerkily through his hair. "Please."

"You won't know. You'll never know." He seemed to be talking to himself. "Whether or not it's real for me, it can never be real for you."

-5-

The students, slumped in various degrees of boredom, occupied the lecture hall's available seats unevenly. Stig had arranged to have an old chalkboard moved from storage, and he wheeled it in front of the modern equipment before each class. He enjoyed the feel of the chalk on his fingers, the staccato tapping as he wrote. A breeze from the windows, propped open by an antiquated crank system, carried the smell of the old building to him and threatened to send him to another time. He resisted and kept talking.

"As you move through time, each particle is continuous. So you see, from the perspective of spacetime, it's not a particle but a thread: unbreakable and woven with all the other threads of matter and energy like a tangled mass of spaghetti. From this perspective, motion is an illusion. It's merely a bend in the thread. Not only are the threads unbreakable, but Einstein showed us that they can only bend so far: the speed of light." As he spoke he drew frantically on the chalkboard to illustrate his point.

"Our brains consist of an immense tangle of these threads. The present is merely the point along them where a particular set of perceptions and thoughts converge. Time does not pass. It is an illusion, an artifact of consciousness."

Stig looked up to see blank expressions on the few students that were still awake, with the exception of one young lady at the back of the class whose hand rose silently.

He squinted his eyes to see the owner of the hand. "Yes. Ms. Verdandi?"

 Not All Those Who Wander Are Lost

"So, if each thread of matter is unbreakable, does that mean that everything is predetermined?"

"No. Because of uncertainty."

"Quantum uncertainty?"

"Bah. Everyone is obsessed with quantum this and quantum that. Flip a coin. There's enough uncertainty in that mundane act to change the course of history." He reached into his pocket, pulled out a coin and prepared to flip it. "There are two possible outcomes. Heads you pass, tails you fail. Do we have a deal?"

"Uh, no. I need an 'A'," she said.

"Couldn't the result of the coin flip be predicted?" another student interjected. "Like, if you knew the location and momentum of every atom in the room?"

"That information is not only unavailable, but unobtainable." Stig flipped the coin, trapping it on the back of his hand. "Even though all the matter and energy in the room consists of unbreakable threads, we now have two possible futures: one where Ms. Verdandi passes and another where she fails. With this simple act I've caused them to branch."

He raised his hand to reveal the coin resting on his palm.

"Dr. Gangleri, I didn't agree to this."

-6-

Dishes clattered as Stig's grandmother gathered them from the table and brought them to the sink. The sound sent shivers of Pavlovian dread down his spine, hollowed him out and filled him with bile. He sat, frozen, at the dinner table, scarcely able to pick at his plate. He had visited this terrible scene too often, in pursuit of the myriad possibilities that sprang from it.

The dinner had been like any other. His grandmother hadn't spoken much during, but at the sink she found the courage to say what had been on her mind the whole time. In a faux casual tone, she spoke over the running water and jangling silverware. "Your mother called today. She says she'll be in town for a day after the holidays. Just a short stopover between movies. She's moving from one set to another clear across the country. Isn't that interesting?" She flashed a quick look at him over her shoulder.

It was one of the rare occasions where his decision didn't matter. Seeing his mother that day stirred a deep pond of sadness and disappointment but had no lasting effect on the timelines. Either way he ended up on the same branch.

"No, I think I'll pass." That wasn't why he had come.

She nodded silently and kept washing. "So, Stiggy, are you all ready for finals?"

"Yes, 'ma."

"You going to get all A's again this year?"

"I always do, 'ma."

"I can't believe you're going to be a junior in college. You grew up so fast."

Stig stared at his plate, pushing peas around with his fork. In some branches he kept eating, slowly finishing his meal while his grandmother cleaned the dishes, but to access certain hidden branches of his possible futures, Yggdrasil demanded a toll, a sacrifice of a not-quite-metaphorical pound of flesh, a price as arbitrary and cruel as most things in life.

With ice in his veins, he stood and carried his plate to the sink. There, he turned on the water, activated the garbage disposal and pushed the remaining food into its roaring maw. The rumble of the disposal changed abruptly to a loud hum and all motion ceased. He looked at the fork, still dangling from his hand. The first time had been an accident, but every time since had been calculated. He stuck it into the drain. The infernal mechanism sprang back to life, jerking the fork from his hand. A blur of motion was followed by an odd coldness in his left eye. Three drops of blood splattered into the sink, one after another, before he felt any pain. The disposal had torn the fork apart and launched a tine into his eye. Reflexively, his hand rose. No matter how many times he went through this, he could not prevent that hand from rising up and making its grisly discovery.

-7-

Stig studied the cracked and peeling plaster of the motel room ceiling. He had spent less than an hour here, but he had done it many times. Did he know the pattern of blemishes any better from his numerous visits? He could have drawn a detailed map of the ceiling after the first time, but it felt familiar now. If Osmond were right, he had imagined each visit here, including this one. But by that logic, the present could be anywhere, even here, and his two-eyed memories as a professor and successful consultant could be the fantasies. This felt real. All the branches did.

"So, where did you see them last?" Carla asked, sitting in her bathrobe beside him on the bed.

"Hmm?"

"Your family. Where was the last place you saw them?"

"It was winter." Stig let the ceiling blur and fade away. "There was a fire in the fireplace. It was actually too warm, but it felt nice. Cozy. My wife lay on the couch. The boys sat on my feet and held onto my legs while I walked around the living room and tousled their hair. I can hear them squealing with laughter and see my wife smiling up at me. So beautiful."

"Huh," she said, uncertain what to make of his story. "That sounds nice."

"Have you ever wondered if the things that are happening to you are real or if you're just imagining them?" he asked.

"Well, I've had some pretty vivid dreams," she said. "You know, where you wake up and it takes a while to figure out it was all a dream. Is that what you mean?"

"I don't think so. I don't know. I never dream."

"Never?"

"Never," he said. "Dreaming is all about forgetting. I don't forget."

"Don't people go crazy if they're not allowed to dream? Maybe that's why things seem unreal to you. You have to be able to forget things that didn't happen to know what did."

"I'm not crazy."

"No, of course not. No. I didn't mean that you were. I just.... Hey, listen, I think I'm going to go take a shower." She stood and looked at him. "We, uh...."

"Yes?"

"We better settle up now. Chances are you'll be gone when I come out."

"Ah. Okay." He rolled over to the side of the bed where his pants lay in a heap, fished around for his wallet, and sat back up. He pulled some bills out and handed them to her.

"So, if I don't see you again, uh, good luck with your family and all that."

"Thanks."

She headed to the bathroom, scooping up her pile of clothes and purse on the way. Just before the bathroom door closed Stig called out.

"Carla."

She stopped and looked back, surprised he knew her name. "Yeah?"

"Don't let Ash play with his cousin next week. His cousin has meningitis. Ash will — he'll get very sick."

Her look of perplexion deepened. "What? How do you know all that?"

"I just do. I, uh, know someone. A doctor told me. It doesn't matter. It's important, though. Okay?"

Visibly shaken by his warning, she gave a slow, "Okay," and closed the bathroom door on her puzzled look.

-8-

"You still with me?" Osmond asked.

Stig sat at the small coffee shop table looking through the window at the busy street outside. He looked up slowly and seemed to rediscover Osmond sitting next to him. "Yeah," he said.

"Well, anyway, I'm sorry," Osmond said.

"Don't be. I understand."

"It's almost as if no one wants to hire a one-eyed guy with no credentials to look over their most precious tech secrets these days, am I right?" Osmond asked with a gentle punch to his friend's shoulder.

"Yeah."

"Seriously, though, have you ever thought about going back to school? Finishing college?"

"Not really."

"Why not?"

"I already did that."

Osmond was puzzled for a second, then understood. "Oh. In other timelines. Right."

"The degrees don't matter," Stig said, staring at the table. "I know everything that the college professor version of me knows. I'm the same person. I've lived both lives. Many lives."

Osmond tapped a finger on the table, trying to think of a polite reply. "The problem is," he said, "other people don't know all that. They don't know what you can do. I mean, I can't even remember all the times you've helped me. Hell, you've saved my life at least twice."

"I'll always help you, Oz. You're my best friend. The year I spent in and out of the hospital after the accident, you never left my side. In all the branches, you're the one constant. I can always count on you."

Osmond put his meaty hand on Stig's back and squeezed his neck. "That was a rough time. Tell you the truth, I didn't think you were going to make it — between the surgeries and the infections." Osmond trailed off shaking his head. "You're lucky to be alive. Anyway, I'm sure our business will take off. We just need a lucky break." He let his arm drop and swirled the dregs of his coffee, lost in thought. When he looked up Stig, was staring out the window again.

"Hey Stig," he said. "Do you think that maybe you could work that mojo of yours to impress some bigwigs? You know, like hold back some CEO just before a piano falls on them, or something like that."

Stig answered without taking his eyes from the street outside. "Maybe."

During their years together, Osmond had grown used to their one-sided conversations. He kind of liked them. He joined Stig in looking out the window, and a longer silence followed, each of them lost in their own thoughts. It was Osmond who once again broke the quiet.

"You know how you always say you're time traveling and I always say you're only daydreaming?"

"Yeah?"

"Well, I was thinking. Have you ever followed one of these branches of yours all the way to the end?"

Stig looked up. "The end?"

"Yeah. I mean, it seems like if you follow any branch of your tree out far enough, you'd eventually die, right?"

"I suppose."

"Well, if you followed a branch all the way to the end and lived to tell about it, wouldn't that prove you're daydreaming and not actually time traveling?"

"I imagine I could leave that branch before I die. Go to another branch."

"Hmm." Osmond scrunched up his face. "I guess. But then that would make you pretty much immortal since you always have another branch you can escape to if you're about to die." Osmond held his arms out dramatically. "I sit in the presence of an immortal, time traveling God."

Osmond saw the serious, thoughtful look on Stig's face and broke out laughing. "I'm teasing you, man."

Stig stared at him blankly.

"You're not," Osmond said.

"Not what?"

"You're not a God. You're just a smart man. So smart that sometimes you're really quite dumb."

Stig just nodded.

"What do you think would happen," Osmond asked, "if you didn't leave a branch before you died?"

"Are you asking me what's after death?"

"Yeah, I guess."

"I don't know."

-9-

"Mr. Gangleri, I can't explain why the antibiotics aren't working, but they aren't. The infection is out of control. The last scan showed a fluid collection eroding through the optic canal. We need to take you to the operating room today to have it drained."

The doctor stood by the door, ready to make a quick getaway. Stig's grandmother sat attentively next to his bed, completely overwhelmed, her spirit broken. Each time he sacrificed his eye to see the branches beyond, he also sacrificed his grandmother's happiness. The sicker he became, the higher the toll she paid. He had seen her in worse shape dozens of times and had buried her as many, but he hated being the cause. Maybe this would be the last time.

"Today?" she asked.

"Yes, we have to try to control the infection. Do you understand, Stig?"

"I do." He understood more than the doctor knew. The antibiotics weren't working because he hadn't been taking them.

The doctor spoke a little longer to his grandmother, had her sign some forms and vanished.

Lying under the glaring surgical lights, Stig waited for the anesthetic to take effect. The morphine barely touched his pain and he shook violently with chills. Each visit to this early bough of Yggdrasil came with multiple surgeries, but he had never been this sick before. He should have been frightened, but instead he just felt exhausted: tired of being separated from the ones he loved and tired of being lost in the tangle of Yggdrasil.

"His blood pressure is dropping," a voice said. He understood the tone, not the words.

The pain faded, and the light grew brighter. The murmuring voices and electromechanical sounds of the room withered like shadows before the advancing light until only silence remained. Silence and light.

He felt himself walking before he saw anything. Walls emerged from the blinding nothingness to form the familiar hallway of his home. He reached the end of the hall and turned the corner hopeful, as always, of what he would find. There, rocking a baby over a bassinet while another slept peacefully nearby, stood his wife. When she saw Stig, a warm smile spread across her face and she lowered the sleeping baby into the bassinet. She hurried across the room and gave him a long hug, burying her head on his shoulder. When they separated she held his face gently and looked into his eyes.

"My love," she said. "You must leave this branch. It ends and your work isn't complete."

"But I finally found you." He took her hands from his face and held them tightly. "I want to stay here, with you."

"Much of Yggdrasil remains undiscovered. Your destiny is unfulfilled," she said. "You must continue."

"I can't leave you. You were too hard to find. What if I never find my way back?"

She laughed gently. "We are easy to find. All branches lead here."

"I don't understand. I've searched Yggdrasil for lifetimes without finding a way here. I shouldn't be here now. This branch — I'm only nineteen and my grandmother still lives in this house. I couldn't have met you yet."

"Silly. You've been looking for us within the tree, but we live beyond the tree of possibilities, in the space between the branches. You've found us here, in this house, because this is familiar to you, but we are not tied to any one time or place. We are always with you, like air against a tree, rippling its leaves and rustling its branches."

"But I've been with you before. How?"

"You caught glimpses of the impossible when your mind was freed."

"From anesthesia? During surgery?"

"Yes. But you must go now, or Yggdrasil will never be complete."

"I don't know where to go. I think I've lost the present. Without it—" He paused and shook his head. "Without it, I can't tell what's real."

"The present is where the future turns into the past. It follows your mind like a mirage. You know this better than anyone."

She released his hands. "Now go, and return to us after you have accomplished great things and grown tired of wandering."

The ebb and flow of chaotic motion outside the coffee shop window mirrored his thoughts, and mesmerized Stig in a way he found hard to resist. Osmond's voice pulled him from his reverie.

"You know how you always say you're time traveling and I always say you're just daydreaming?"

"Yeah?"

"Well, I was thinking. Have you ever followed a branch out to the end?"

"No. Not to the end. But close enough to see what's beyond."

"Oh?" Osmond looked surprised. "What's there? What did you see?"

Stig looked up from the window and smiled. "The impossible."

See Douglas Anstruther's story "Not All Those Who Wander Are Lost" online at Metaphorosis. If you liked it, leave a comment. Authors love that!
Remember to subscribe to our e-mail updates so you'll know when new stories are posted.

About the story

I wanted to explore the idea that perfect prediction of the future could be confused with, and possibly be indistinguishable from, actually experiencing the future. As I wrote, I discovered that for someone with the ability to do this, the concept of the present became less relevant, and along with it, the notion of mortality.

In addition to the intentionally unanswered questions of whether or not Stig is really immortal and whether or not a real, objective present exists that he has lost, the story raised other questions along the way. I wasn't able to address these in the short story format and they were better left to the reader's imagination anyway. For example: If Stig's mental facilities are impaired (from drugs or sleep) does he lose his ability to jump away from danger? Is there some sort of meta-time that allows the linear progression of Stig's own experiences? If he doesn't go back to a thread, does time pass on it? If there were two people with the same ability, could either one extend the same thread? I do hope that the list goes on and that many more questions are raised among readers.

A question for the author

Q: If someone wanted to make an animated series out of your work, based on the title or recurring themes, what would it look like?

A: There are a few times in the story when the present isn't holding Stig's attention very well and we find him spacing out. Is he considering a leap to another branch? Maybe he's moved on to another timeline and is letting the one we see coast on autopilot.

An animated series could show these other timelines in the background, constantly impinging on his attention, threatening to carry him away, competing with each other to be his next destination and coloring his decisions and mood with knowledge of alternate histories and futures that the people around him haven't experienced. It'd look pretty trippy.

Also, dark. I like my animated series dark.

About the author

Douglas Anstruther was raised among the long cold winters of Minnesota. At age seven he discovered that there were other worlds beyond our own and was astonished, and frankly disappointed, that no one had thought this important enough to mention earlier - a sentiment he still holds today. At some point he married his lovely wife, Dana, went to medical school, had three very nearly perfect children and moved to Wilmington, North Carolina. When not tending to people's kidneys, Douglas likes to read, write and talk about history, linguistics, space, AIs, the singularity, and everything in between. He particularly enjoys writing stories that will rattle around in the readers' head for a while after the last page has been turned.

www.facebook.com/douglasanstruther, @DouglsAnstruthr

Copyright

Copyright 2018, Metaphorosis Publishing

Cover art © 2018 by Julia Naurzalieva

"The Bagel Shop Owner's Nephew" © 2018, J. Tynan Burke

"Upon the Fallen Leaves of the Gingko Tree" © 2018, Mads Alvey

"Just a Fire" © 2018, A. Martine

"All the Colors I Cannot See" © 2018, L'Erin Ogle

"Not All Those Who Wander Are Lost" © 2018, Douglas Anstruther

Authors also retain copyrights to all other material in the anthology.

Metaphorosis Publishing

Metaphorosis offers beautifully written science fiction and fantasy. Our projects include:

Metaphorosis Magazine

Metaphorosis, a weekly magazine of SFF short stories, including stories from all the authors in this anthology. Find out more at magazine.metaphorosis.com, and sign up to be notified of new stories.

Metaphorosis Books

Recent books from Metaphorosis can be found at <u>books.metaphorosis.com</u>, and include:

Metaphorosis 2017

Metaphorosis 2016

All the stories from *Metaphorosis* magazine's second year.

Almost all the stories from *Metaphorosis* magazine's first year.

Metaphorosis: Best of 2017

The best science fiction and fantasy stories from *Metaphorosis'* 2nd year.

Metaphorosis: Best of 2016

The best science fiction and fantasy stories from *Metaphorosis'* 1st year.

Reading 5X5

Five stories, five times

Twenty-five SFF authors, five base stories, five versions of each – see how different writers take on the same material.

Reading 5X5

Writers' Edition

All the stories from the regular, readers' edition, plus two extra stories, the story seed, and authors' notes.

Best Vegan SFF of 2017

The best vegan science fiction and fantasy stories of 2017!

Best Vegan SFF of 2016

The best vegan science fiction and fantasy stories of 2016!

Susurrus

A darkly romantic story of magic, love, and suffering.

www.ingramcontent.com/pod-product-compliance
Lightning Source LLC
Chambersburg PA
CBHW020516120726
47904CB00003B/858